BOY GIANT

Son of Gulliver

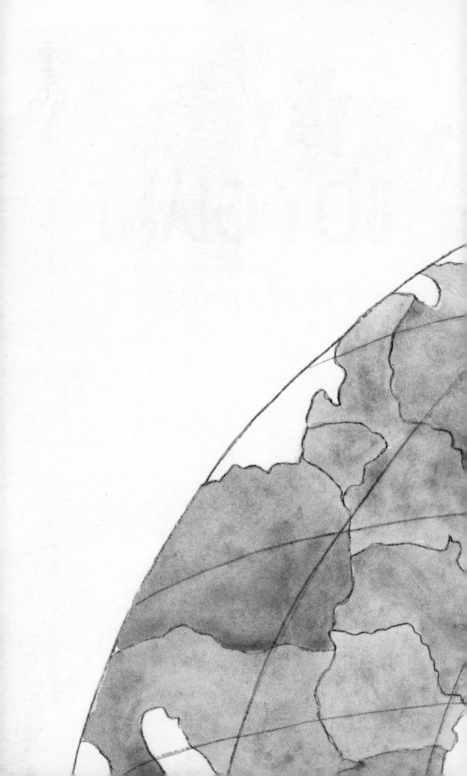

Also by Michael Morpurgo

michael morpurgo

BOY GIANT

Son of Gulliver

illustrated by Michael Foreman

HarperCollins *Children's Books*

First published in Great Britain by
HarperCollins *Children's Books* in 2019
HarperCollins *Children's Books* is a division of HarperCollins*Publishers* Ltd,
HarperCollins Publishers
1 London Bridge Street
London SE1 9GF

The HarperCollins website address is:
www.harpercollins.co.uk

1

HB ISBN 978-0-00-834791-8
TPB ISBN 978-0-00-834792-5

Michael Morpurgo and Michael Foreman assert the moral right to be
identified as the author and illustrator of the work respectively.

Typeset in Bell MT point 12/20
Printed and bound in England by CPI Group (UK) Ltd, Croydon, CR0 4YY

MIX
Paper from
responsible sources
FSC™ C007454
www.fsc.org

This book is produced from independently certified FSC™ paper
to ensure responsible forest management.

For more information visit: www.harpercollins.co.uk/green

For Tom and Kate,
and for Hannah, Jack and Zoe.
M.M.

To my big brothers,
Ivan and Pud,
giants of my boyhood.
M.F.

With thanks to Jonathan Swift, author of the great *Gulliver's Travels*, published on 28 October 1726.

Thanks also to Clare, Michael Foreman, Vicki Berwick, Nick Lake and Ann-Janine Murtagh for their help in making this book happen.

And also my thanks to Sarah Outen, ocean rower extraordinaire, and an inspiration to us all.

'Be not inhospitable to strangers lest they be angels in disguise'

George Whitman

CONTENTS

First Part

Second Part

Third Part

Fourth Part

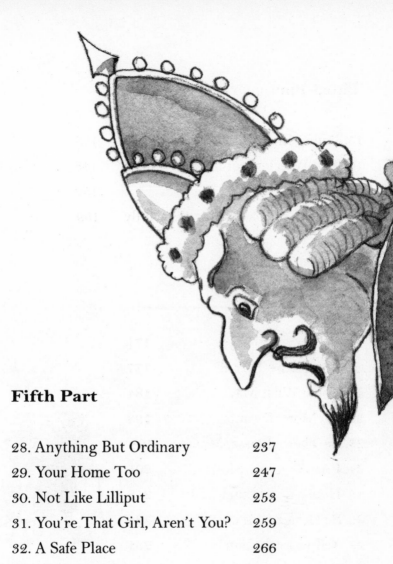

Fifth Part

FIRST
Part

CHAPTER ONE

Tiny, They Called Me

All we knew about her was that she called herself J.J.,
that she spoke English, that she was alone out there in
her big yellow rowing boat and that she was like a giant
to all three of us – even me – a giant with a bandaged
wrist and plasters on her fingers.

'So tell me,' she said, 'tell me everything.'

I could hardly refuse, could I? I mean, this J.J. had
saved our lives. It was thanks only to this stranger that
we were dry again, well fed, warm and rested.

'I mean,' she went on, 'I want to know how it is that
you're out here on the open ocean in such a small boat.
Who are you? Where have you come from?'

I could have asked her much the same questions. But I found myself telling her our whole story. I was happy to tell her too, not just because she had shown us such kindness, but because once I began telling her our story out loud, it somehow helped me to believe it had all really happened to me, helped me to remember who I was, who I had become. That she would believe me I had no doubt. After all, she had the evidence right in front of her. She could hardly take her eyes off the evidence. The three of us were there to prove it. We were the truth of our own story.

I began at the beginning, because without the beginning none of it would have made sense to her; and anyway, none of it would ever have happened. I would never have had to leave home, and my life would have been another story altogether.

'It's quite a long story,' I told her.

'That's fine,' she said. 'I need to rest this wrist anyway. Can't row far like this.'

So I began.

*

Where I come from is no longer my home. There was a house and a village I once called my home, in Afghanistan. I had a family of my own once. Not any more. I have my name – Omar – and I have Mother, but I don't know where she is. I think and I hope she may be in England with Uncle Said. I was on my way to find her. That's why we were out here on our little boat when you found us, and we found you.

I don't know any more what day or month or year it is, but I think I must now be about sixteen years old. Of my beginnings, of my home, there is not much to tell, and I do not like to speak of it or think of it, because it makes me sad to remember. My home was a quiet place, in

a peaceful town in the countryside. We lived on the
edge of town. My father was a shepherd, our flock
was our livelihood. We never went hungry or thirsty.
I had a little sister, Hanan. She and I were much loved
in our home. We were together. We were all happy.

School was school. All my friends were there. We
learnt our lessons, played together. But I was always
small and thin, and at school I was never allowed to
forget it. 'Tiny', they called me. Little I may have
been, but I was by far the best at cricket. No one hit

the ball harder. No one bowled faster. The pitch was
always bumpy, but it was the same for us all, and it
was fine. Everything was fine. I could read the bounce
of every ball they bowled at me, see it on to the bat.
I lived for my cricket, and my family. Everything was
good – well, mostly.

Every night I went to sleep wishing I would score
more runs the next day or take more wickets, and
I prayed I would be a little taller in the morning. I
would measure myself against the mark Mother had

made on the wall. The next day I would often score more runs, or take more wickets, or both, but I was never any taller. Hanan was still taller than me every morning and she was two years younger than me.

Then the war came to our town and I had other worries, more serious worries. I do not know to this day why the war came. It was on the morning of my

tenth birthday, I remember. We heard the planes in the sky, and then the bombing began. We were in school. There was nowhere to hide, nowhere to run to. At the end of that day our home was in ruins, our school too. Many of my friends had died. I was there when they were buried. I helped to bury them. Father died too, when the planes came again the next morning,

and so did most of our sheep. Then we discovered Hanan was missing. We looked and we called, but we never found her. Only Mother and I were left. We had nothing, no shelter, no food, no father, no sister, no daughter.

The aid workers came after that, and they brought us food and tents, and built us a refugee camp. We weren't a family any more. We were refugees. We lived in that camp a long time. The aid workers were from England, and they were kind to us. They smiled at us, and we liked that. It cheered our hearts. There were doctors and nurses, who were good to us. It was cold through that winter, but we survived. The refugee camp was never a home for us. It was a place of shelter – that's all. Sometimes we played football and cricket with the aid workers, and they taught me to speak a little English. They were amazed at how good I was at cricket. I liked to amaze them. It made them smile.

But then one day Mother said it was not safe for us to stay, that she was sure the planes would come again, or the soldiers. Many in the camp had decided to leave, and we would go with them.

So Mother and I, and a few others, we left the camp in the middle of the night and began to walk. We walked for weeks and weeks. We walked over the mountains, through the desert, followed where others went, all of us with only one thing on our minds. To find somewhere far away from the war, anywhere, that was a place of peace where there was food and water and shelter, where we could be safe. How long and how far we walked I do not know.

Sleep was our only comfort. You can forget when you are asleep. Waking up was the worst part of every day. I wanted only to stay where I was, curled up on the ground, and never get up again. I was so tired, too tired to care any more.

Mother saved my life every morning. She would never let me lie there. She always said that if I didn't get up, and walk on, I would die, and she wasn't going to let that happen. She would tell me sometimes that

she could smell the sea, that I had to be strong and brave, like Father and Hanan had been. She promised me that beside the sea there would be a boat waiting for us, to carry us to safety, to a new life in a new home where there would be lots of smiling people like the aid workers and doctors and nurses in the camp, and where there was no more war and no bombing. All I had to do, Mother said, was to put one foot in front of the other. Her love and her promises were all that kept me walking.

There were wire fences, there were lorries, there were trains, there were more refugee camps. The police beat us. There were people who yelled at us to go home, others who took us in and fed us and gave us warm clothes, and smiled at us. We never knew what to expect.

But Mother and me, we put one foot in front of the other, and we walked.

CHAPTER TWO

Fore Street, Mevagissey

Sure enough, after a year or more of wandering, one day we came over a hill, and there – just as Mother had promised – was the sea, and some houses and people, and, like a miracle, there was the boat waiting for us. Mother told me, her arm around me, that God was good to us, and that I should always believe that.

She had little enough left to sell, the bracelets on her arms, the rings on her fingers. They were enough to pay the men to allow me on to their boat, but not Mother. None of her tears, nor mine, were enough to persuade them to let her go with me.

I had to go on alone, she told me. She would follow

on later. We would find one another in England. She promised me faithfully. And Mother always keeps her promises.

I remember her last words to me. 'Go to your Uncle Said in his café in Mevagissey,' she told me. 'Fore Street. Mevagissey. Remember, Fore Street. Remember, Mevagissey. Say it over and over in your head, Omar, so that you do not ever forget. Fore Street, Mevagissey. Fore Street, Mevagissey. Wait for me there. I will come. Go now, Omar. Say to the people in England that you are his nephew, and they will let you stay. Uncle Said told me they would do this. Tell them where he lives, where he works in his café. They will let you stay with him. Do not worry. They will have smiling eyes, and there is no war there either. This way you will live, and if you live, so will I. We will meet again, we will, God willing.'

I clung to her. I cried into her.

She whispered in my ear that she loved me more than life itself, but I had to be a man now like Father had been, that I had to be brave like Hanan, that I was to go and cry no more. 'Smile for me,' she said, 'so I will remember you this way.' I tried, tried so hard, but I did not succeed. My tears would not let me.

The last time I saw Mother she was standing there on the shore watching the boat take me away. She was becoming smaller before my eyes. Soon she was not there at all, and then nor was the shore.

I was in a big rubber boat with an engine that coughed and spluttered. The boat was so full of people that it was difficult for all of us to find anywhere to sit down. To begin with the sea was calm about us, lapping but calm. People were telling one another that it wasn't far, that it was a good boat, that we would soon be there, soon be safe.

I had seen the sea in photographs, on films, and it had always been blue. But this sea was not blue. It was grey, and wide, and darkening, and threatening, and seemed to go on forever into the distance, where it became sky, a sky that was as grey as the sea.

I do not know how many nights and days I spent on that boat. I found at last a place to sit on the side. There I passed the long cold hours, trying all the while to calm my fears. I made myself imagine Mevagissey, the place where I was going. I tried to think of Uncle Said in his café in England. I had never met him. I had seen his photograph, the one Mother kept with her all the time. I had spoken to him only once, a long time before, on Skype. But then he was pixelated, so I could not see him at all well. I could tell that he had a moustache, and not much else. I remember his voice quite well, though. He told me I should come to see him one day, and help him in his café.

'I'm coming, Uncle Said!' I shouted out loud. 'Fore Street, Mevagissey! Fore Street, Mevagissey!' Some people around me on that boat looked at me as if I had gone mad. But I didn't mind what they thought. I was going to Mevagissey! Fore Street, Mevagissey!

CHAPTER THREE

Something to Cling On To

Mevagissey, Fore Street, Mevagissey. I kept saying those words out loud to myself on the boat, so I should never forget them, but also because I wanted to practise them. I practised all the English words I knew, that the aid workers had taught me: Hello, son. Goal! Foul! Chocolate. High five! Manchester United. Chelsea. Goodbye. See you. Come back soon. And of course all the cricket words I knew, like: bowler, batsman, over, wicket, out, not out, four, six and owzat!

Owzat was my favourite word. It cheered me up every time I said it. I wanted to speak as many

English words as I could before I arrived in England. I wanted to show off to Mother, when I saw her, how well I could speak English. And practising my English words kept my mind off the sea and the waves and the cold and sound of all the moaning and crying around me in the boat.

Hope kept me going too. I hoped everyone in England would be smiling as Mother had said they would be. I hoped we would be happy there, and safe. Just thinking about it made me happy. I would have a home again and go to school, have friends again, play cricket again. I tried only to think most about Uncle Said, and cricket, not of Mother, not of Father or Hanan. I knew that if I thought of Mother too much I would cry. And I would not cry. I wanted to be a man, like Father had been. I wanted to be brave as Hanan had been. Father had never cried. Hanan would not cry. So I would not cry.

Within a few days the last of any drinking water was gone. The engine had long since broken down. There were waves now that towered over us, and with them always a biting wind. Sitting up on the side was no longer safe. I sat huddled now with the others in the bottom of the boat. The cold shivered me, numbed my hands and feet. All around me there was crying and whimpering and praying. I could see − we all could see − that all the time the boat was lower and lower in the sea. With every wave, more seawater was coming over the side. Some of us cupped our hands and did our best to bail it out. But the water was filling the boat faster than we could get rid of it.

In the end we gave up. We were sitting in water, lying in it, many of us more dead than alive. Every one of us there realised by now that soon enough we would all be drowning in it. We knew that no help was going to come. The boat was filling up, and I could not swim. None of us could swim. They prayed to God. I prayed to God, and I tried to think of Mother and Uncle Said, of how wonderful it would be to live with them in Fore Street, Mevagissey. Fore Street, Mevagissey.

The great storm came at night, the waves tossing us, each of them trying harder than the one before to lift the boat up and flip us over. The sea was playing with the boat, playing with us, teasing us before it drowned us and swallowed us up forever. Too weak now, unable to hold on, all of us helpless, we were being thrown one by one out of the boat.

I knew my turn had to come soon. There was crying and screaming all about me. I had no hope left of ever seeing Mother again, no hope of seeing Uncle Said or Fore Street, Mevagissey.

Lying there in the water at the bottom of the boat, I remember reaching out for something, anything to cling on to, so that I would not be tossed out by the next big wave, when my hand found a piece of rope

under the water. I grasped it, pulled and pulled at it.
It was long, but at last it held firm. I managed to tie it
around my waist, and I lay there, praying for Mother,
praying for me.

In the end I was too cold and too exhausted to even pray. Darkness was closing around me. I knew I would never see morning. I did not care any more. I gave myself up to the darkness and the cold and thought only of Mother and Father and Hanan. I promised myself I would think of them till my last breath. That way we could all be together at the end.

CHAPTER FOUR

The Little People

I must have fallen into sleep, because next thing I knew, I found myself waking up.

The storm had passed. There was the warmth of sunlight on my face, and I could hear a sound of chattering and whispering, like the murmuring of a flock of birds flying about me. But I could see no birds. I realised then that I was no longer lying in the boat at all, that the sea was no longer surging beneath me. I was on land, dry land. I could feel it under me. I tried to move my head, to discover where I was, but I could not move it. My arms would not move either, nor my legs. All I could move were my fingers. I clutched at the ground beneath them. It felt as if I was clawing at sand. I must be on a beach somewhere. But I had no idea where I was. I did not care. I was alive! I had survived.

I discovered I could wriggle my toes. But try as I did, I could not find the strength even to lift my head to see them. I could swivel my eyes, but my neck I could not move however hard I tried. I was overwhelmed by terror, and I was shivering uncontrollably, yet I did not feel cold. I did not feel anything. This was what the beginning of dying was like, I thought.

In my panic, I cried out, calling for help, louder and louder, until my throat ached with it. Hearing myself at least lifted my spirits. If my voice worked and my throat ached, then that must be good. I was still alive. There was hope. But I knew I needed help. I could hear the waves tumbling on to the sand not too far away, they were rushing up towards me, every wave coming closer. I feared the worst. Sooner or later the sea would reach me, and then cover me. I had to find a way to move or I would drown. I shouted for help again, and again. But no one came.

I did hear that strange whispering again, and a chirruping and a chattering like a flock of thousands of birds gathering to roost at sunset. It was a sound that reminded me of evenings at home when we were out playing cricket in the last of the daylight. My hearing worked, and my memory worked. I could see the sun, and the sky. My seeing worked too. And there was more feeling now in my legs and feet. Every new sign of life in me gave me hope.

I felt something tickling my toe, then crawling up my leg. An insect, I thought, a scorpion maybe and it might sting me. But I didn't mind. I could feel it. I could feel it.

I heard that whispering sound again. It wasn't bird noise after all, but voices, small voices. I thought at first in my muddled head that these might be scorpions talking. I tried again to lift my head to see, and still could not move it. Then I was drifting away, down into a deep sleep. It was a comfortable sleep, a warm sleep. There was no more shivering. If this was dying then I did not mind a bit, not any more.

I woke to more whispering and murmuring. It was certainly not birds, I decided, nor was it the hush of waves washing back over the sand into the sea. It was not birds. It was not waves. It was people, lots of them, and they were speaking in small voices, voices that were all around me. When I tried to lift my head now, I found to my surprise I could do it, just a little, just enough.

Then I felt something on the forefinger of my right hand. I looked down, expecting to see a scorpion. Instead, there was a little man there, standing on my finger. Minute he was, too small to be real, I thought. He was wearing a three-cornered hat, a long coat, and he had buckles on his shoes. I never saw anyone dressed like this before. I imagined at first I must be dreaming. But then I knew I wasn't asleep. I could smell the sea, and there were clouds in the sky, and

birds, white birds flying above me, crying and cawing. I could feel the breeze on my face. None of this was imagined, none of this was a dream, and nor were the crowds of little people I could now see all over the beach, nor were the horses and carts imagined, nor were the little coloured blankets that I saw covering me like patchwork from my ankles up to my chest. The little man standing now in the palm of my open hand might have been no bigger than my little finger. But he was real. I was not imagining him. This was not a dream.

He was helping a little old lady up on to my hand, and then they were both making their way slowly up my arm and over my shoulder and across my chest, towards the point of my chin. The little old lady was walking with a stick and wore a long blue dress and feathers in her hat. They stood there together side by side, peering down in silence at me for a long while.

And when she spoke it was in a thin tremulous voice, which reminded me at once of how my grandmother's voice had been. There was hushed silence all around me. Everyone was listening. I had no idea to begin with what she was saying to me. But then I began to recognise a word here, and a word there. The sound of the language was oddly familiar. It was how the aid workers in the camp used to speak. The little old lady was definitely speaking English. Her tone was warm, and hospitable, so I presumed this must be a speech of greeting, like an elder back home in my town might have given to a visitor. I could tell that she was assuming I understood every word she was saying, which I was not.

CHAPTER FIVE

Me, a Mountain!

When the little old woman had finished speaking everyone clapped, and the children amongst them were jumping up and down cheering wildly.

A thousand thoughts were running through my mind and none of them made any sense. Was all this really happening to me? My shivering had stopped entirely. My whole body was tingling now with life, warmth and feeling. The old lady standing before me was breathing hard after the exertions of her speech, leaning heavily on her stick. I did not know what to say, but I felt I had to say something, that it was expected. The silence all around me told me that much. But I was struck dumb, still trying to take it all in, to believe what I was seeing. These people were all living, breathing creatures, but all were impossibly small, and dressed like no one I had ever seen before. They were real, as real as I was. So if they were real, and if they all spoke English, I thought, then maybe I had been washed up in England. But the aid workers that I had got to know near my town in Afghanistan were not small like these people, and neither did they dress like them.

I decided to try on them some of my English words I knew, to be sure I was right, that they did really speak English. I tried cricket words, then some words the aid workers had taught me. 'Owzat,' I said. 'Not out, high five, hello, goodbye, chocolate, see you, doctor, you all right, son?'

No one seemed to be understanding a word I was saying. So I tried something else, the only other English words I could think of, hopeful that maybe they would know where it was. 'Fore Street, Mevagissey. Fore Street, Mevagissey.'

They just looked at me, bewildered.

I tried again, louder this time. 'Mevagissey! Mevagissey! Fore Street . . . Four! Six!' The numbers did it.

I saw sudden recognition on the faces all around me and some alarm too. Perhaps I had spoken too loudly, I thought. I tried the same words again, softer this time, and then a few different words to see if they would understand. 'Football. Manchester United. Chelsea. Joe Root. England. Afghanistan.'

The more I said, the less surprised they were looking, but the more puzzled and amused they became. They were whispering amongst each other, and some were laughing. Encouraged by this I tried again, and soon they were all laughing. 'Fore Street, Mevagissey! Chocolate! Owzat!' They particularly seemed to love it when I said 'owzat'. So much so they were echoing it back to me.

'Owzat! Owzat!'

But then I noticed that the old lady was not laughing any more, not smiling either. She was standing there staring at me. I had the strange feeling that she was not just trying to work out who I was, and where I had come from, but she was trying to remember me, to *remember* who I was. It was as if she thought that she recognised me, which I knew was not possible. Anyway, with some difficulty, and helped by her companion, she turned away from me, and made her way along my arm, over my hand and back down on to the sand. I watched her being led across the beach to a rock not far away. There she sat down, her hands folded in her lap, looking up at me, her eyes never leaving my face.

Meanwhile, the little people, led by the children, were crowding all around me, reaching out to touch my feet, my hands, my clothes. I was being examined, investigated. Then, more confident now, they were beginning to clamber up on to me. I did not feel in the least threatened by them. I could tell they meant me no harm. It didn't seem to be in their nature. The girls and boys amongst them were much more daring than the grown-ups, and were already all over me, shinning easily up every nook and cranny of me. I was thinking that I must have been like a mountain to them.

'Me? A mountain?' I laughed aloud at the thought of it. Little Omar was a mountain! Tiny was a mountain! If my friends could see me now. If Mother could see me now! Oh how I wished Mother could see me now.

Then they were pulling all the blankets off me, and rubbing me vigorously all over. I lay back and closed my eyes as the blessed warmth flooded me from the tips of my toes to the roots of my hair. These little people were bringing me back to life.

I started to hum. Maybe it was because I was reminded of the comfort and warmth I remembered as a small boy at bedtime when Mother had held me close and sung to me. It was her song that came back to me then, her lullaby, that I found myself humming.

After a while they began to hum along with me, and I loved that. I knew then for sure that I was amongst friends, and safe at last. Exhaustion and relief, the rhythm of the waves lapping on the beach and the sound of Mother's tune in my head must have been enough to send me off to sleep again.

But I did not sleep for long. I felt my eyelids being prised open. The children had decided to wake me. I woke to find hundreds of these little people crawling all over me. Some were doing handstands and backflips, some had taken to tumbling off me for fun, and then climbing back up again.

Down the beach I saw that the old woman was still sitting on her rock, her companion beside her. A few others were gathering around her, and kept glancing back up at me as she was talking to them.

After some time the old lady at last got to her feet and began to walk up the beach towards me, her companion holding her elbow to steady her as she came. The children were called away. They jumped down off me, some of them reluctantly, and were soon standing in amongst the grown-ups, quietened down and waiting. I felt something important was about to happen.

I raised myself up on to my elbows. A silence had fallen over the beach. They were all looking expectantly at the old lady now, as I was too. For long moments she said nothing. Then, as she came closer, I saw that there were tears in her eyes, and I could see now that they were tears of recognition.

'Gulliver,' she said softly, pointing her stick up at me. Then louder, and louder, 'Gulliver?' she cried. 'Gulliver?'

CHAPTER SIX

Son of Gulliver

What 'Gulliver' meant I had no idea. Not then, anyway.

But from the way the old lady was talking and the way she was looking at me, the way they were all looking at me, I had the distinct feeling that I really was being welcomed *home*, as if I was some long-lost relative. The more I thought about it, the more I was sure that was who they believed I was. I must be 'Gulliver' – I was someone they all already knew and loved.

'Gulliver! Gulliver!'

They were all shouting it out now, chanting it. I was some kind of a hero to these little people, to the children especially. Who they thought I was I could not imagine, nor did that bother me at all. I was quite happy to bask in such a joyous welcome. I responded by lifting my hands in the air and waving to them, which caused them to cheer and shout even louder. And then in amongst the chants of 'Gulliver! Gulliver!' I began to hear 'Welcome, Gulliver. Owzat! Owzat!'

The more they chanted, the more I was sure they were using English words, spoken differently maybe, but definitely English words. It was the language of cricket, the language of aid workers in the camp. So,

getting to my feet – and I was still unsteady at first –
I raised my arms again and chanted back at them,
'Gulliver! Gulliver! Owzat! Owzat!'

And then I thought of another word the aid
workers in the refugee camp had taught me. 'Hello!' I
shouted back. 'Hello!'

I could tell from the delight on their faces that
this was a word they knew, that they recognised, an
English word. So this had to be England! And if I was
in England, then Uncle Said and his café might not be
far away. Mevagissey was not far away.

These people may be little, I thought, and all the doctors and aid workers I had known had been giants compared to them. But you could have ordinary-sized people and tiny people living in England, in the same country, couldn't you? *Why not?* I told myself. I had arrived! I was safe and I was in England, where Mother had promised we would be. I had only to wait for her here, as she had said. Mother had been right about something else too. These English people were smiling people, welcoming people.

I was filled with relief, bursting with happiness. I punched the air again and again and cried out, 'Owzat! Owzat!'

The tiny people were joining in, echoing every word. 'Fore Street! Mevagissey! Four! Six! Not out! High five!'

Whenever I shouted out, punching the air, the name they had given me – 'Gulliver! Gulliver!' – they went wild. And they went wilder still when I began chanting 'Owzat! Owzat!'

But then I noticed that the old lady was not joining

in all this excitement. She was sitting there on her rock, looking up at me, her brow furrowed. She got to her feet then, and began to walk towards me, on the arm of her companion. I crouched down to be closer to her, holding out my hand in friendship. I was worried I had angered her somehow, and wanted to make it up to her.

She said nothing for a while, but was looking at me long and hard. Then she reached out and took my finger, gently drawing my hand towards her, so that she and her companion could step up on to it. Once they were balanced, I lifted them up very carefully, keeping my hand steady, so that they would not fall over. We were face to face now. The crowd had fallen quite silent.

The old lady and her companion were standing side by side in the palm of my hand. There was no fear in their eyes, only intense curiosity. Beckoning me closer she reached out her hand to touch my face. Then she was brushing the hair away from my forehead. A sudden smile came over her.

'Not Gulliver,' she said softly. 'Son of Gulliver.' Then she turned and proclaimed it out loud to the crowd. 'Son of Gulliver! He is Son of Gulliver!'

There was a gasp of amazement at this, from all around. So now I was a son of this Gulliver. And I knew what 'son' meant. One of the aid workers in the refugee camp – Jimbo he was called – had shown me photographs on his phone of a boy about my age, obviously his son, holding a cricket bat – he liked cricket too, and Jimbo was the one who used to call me 'son'. 'Hello, son,' he'd say to me sometimes. 'You all right, son?'

So now I was 'Son of Gulliver'. I could think of nothing else to do but look as pleased as the old lady was, as her companion was, as everyone seemed to be. I called out, 'Son of Gulliver! Son of Gulliver! Owzat!'

The old lady seemed happy with that. They all were, so I thought I must have said the right thing.

From then on, that's who I was to these people, 'Son of Gulliver!' But the children usually preferred to call me Owzat. I still did not understand who

Gulliver was, nor why I should be his son. That, and everything else about this strange place, which had to be England – I was sure of it by now – was still a complete mystery to me. But I did not mind this, nor how confusing and strange everything was.

Another confusion was the language they spoke. I had already heard many of them speaking amongst themselves in another language that did not sound at all like English. So they must speak in two languages. Strange again, but what did it matter? All I knew was that I was amongst people who were kind, and I was safe. What else could matter?

But something else did matter. I was suddenly feeling weak with hunger and I was dying of thirst.

CHAPTER SEVEN

The Whole World

It was as if the old lady could read my mind. At that very moment she clapped her hands, and at once everyone seemed to know exactly what to do. Within moments they were all fetching and carrying, all the horses and carts on the beach were on the move, and the little people, children too, were busily unloading them.

They reminded me of the armies of ants on the march that I had often watched back home in my town. Every one of these little people seemed to have a task to do, and they all understood their part in it.

The task, I was very pleased to see, was to bring me all the food and water I could ever have wanted.

Once I had lowered the old lady and her companion down on to the sand again, I watched as the little

people brought me fish and bread and grapes and nuts, all I could eat, and some berries and then some water, which came in barrels too. A barrel of water was no more than a mouthful to me, but there were lots of barrels, and they kept coming, and I kept drinking.

They came and laid at my feet all the food and drink I needed. And I needed a great deal. They never once tired and every one of them would say something in greeting as they presented me with yet another gift of some fish or a grape or a barrel of water. 'Hello, Son of Gulliver,' or 'Owzat!' or 'Welcome.'

I saw such a kindness and open-hearted generosity in their eyes. I could not help thinking what a difference this was from the other world I had left behind me, from the world of suffering, and sadness, from the ruined town that had once been my home, from the family and friends I had lost, from the sprawling refugee camp where we had to live. How strange it was to be surrounded now by all this warmth and loving care and attention. How I wished Mother and Hanan and Father could be here with me to see how good and kind people could be.

I thought then of Mother standing there on the shore watching me leave in that overcrowded boat, and my mind went back to the terrible journey across the sea, the fear that had gripped my heart, the cold in my bones, the endless skies, the endless sea, the frantic efforts we had made to save ourselves, to bail that water out from the bottom of the boat, cupping our frozen hands and scooping out what we could, but watching helpless and, as the waves came again over the side, how the boat had sunk lower and lower into the water, and how one by one the others who had been with me were no longer there, how I had been left on my own, lying in the cold of the water for days and nights on end praying to be saved, calling out for Mother, and keeping her last words in my head, the words she told me never to forget, 'Fore Street, Mevagissey'.

Without my meaning to, those words spoke themselves out loud again on the beach in front of all the little people. 'Fore Street, Mevagissey. Fore Street, Mevagissey.'

I began to cry then, whether in grief or relief or joy I did not know. I do know that many a little hand reached and tried to comfort me, and I remember that brought me such joy and helped drive away my sorrows and in time stopped my tears. I had food, drink, and hundreds of little friends, I thought.

What more could I need? I was safe with these little people, safe at last, and for some reason much loved too. And that meant the world to me, the whole world.

CHAPTER EIGHT

Gran Baruta

When I think back now, I am amazed at how even on that first day I came to feel so much at home amongst these little people, and how soon any barriers of language and culture, and indeed of size, were broken down. In large part this was due to the old lady, Gran Baruta, clearly the matriarch of these people, like a grandmother to all of them. She was the one who made me feel that I belonged.

I soon learnt that her constant companion was her grandson, Tapit, and that all old people here had just such a young companion at their side. The young looked after the old, and the old looked after the young. I was already beginning to learn that was how it was here, that it was how these little people lived, for one another.

Tapit was amongst the tallest of the little people, but even so I must have been at least twenty times or thirty times the size of him. I towered over him, over Gran Baruta, over everyone and everything – the horses, the boats, the trees, the animals, the fields and the rivers. Everything on this island seemed to be in proportion to the miniscule size of its inhabitants.

Tapit was as welcoming and kind to me as all the others. But I think this was mostly because of his grandmother, Gran Baruta, and her fondness for this

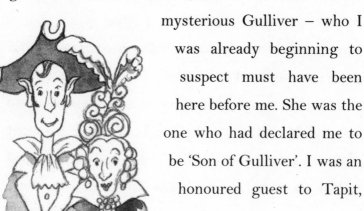 mysterious Gulliver – who I was already beginning to suspect must have been here before me. She was the one who had declared me to be 'Son of Gulliver'. I was an honoured guest to Tapit,

and to everyone, because of her, and because of this Gulliver person who was still a mystery to me.

Very quickly, even on that first day, I was becoming accustomed to the size of these little people, but in all the time I was with them, I never got over how wonderful it was for me, for Tiny Omar, to be so huge, to be able to look down at all of them. Yet despite my size, they did not fear me. They knew that I was not a threat to them. Otherwise why did they not all run away in terror at the sight of me? No, they assumed I was gentle, harmless, and as kind as they were. I was sure this might be because of the Gulliver who had come before me – he had obviously been much loved. I was longing to know more about him.

When I stood up again, with all these miniscule people gazing up at me, and wondering open-mouthed at how high I was, I had the first real opportunity to look around, not so much at the little people, now, but at all the country on whose shores I had been washed up, the country I knew must be England.

I climbed to the very top of the dunes, taking the
greatest care not to tread on any of the little people,
nor on their horses and their carts. From there I

could see that there was sea all around me, that I
was on a small island, horseshoe-like in shape, with
woods and fields and rivers. There were sheep and

cows and horses in the fields, and I could see a village where the narrow streets led down to a harbour full of boats. There were sandy beaches, gently shelving dunes, similar to the one I was standing on; and over the sea, in the distance, another island. At the far end of my island, at one end of the horseshoe, I saw a rocky mountain that rose steeply from the plain. I imagined there must be sheer cliffs on the other side. I remembered then that Mother had told me – or perhaps it had been Jimbo in the refugee camp – that England was an island. So that village I could see now, not far away, might be Mevagissey! I was so close!

I was longing to find out, to explore, and would have set off at once, but Gran Baruta and Tapit had other ideas, and were waving at me, beckoning me to come down off the dunes. When I came closer she called up to me, trying to tell me something. I could not understand her. Tapit was lying down on the sand at my feet, clearly acting out for me what she wanted me to do. I had no idea why they wanted me to lie down, but I did it anyway. I lay back on the warm sand and waited for whatever was to happen. I knew these people meant me no harm, and that anyway they were far too small to hurt me. I was quite content to lie there, bask in the sun and close my eyes.

For some while nothing at all seemed to happen. Half asleep by now I lifted my head once or twice to see what was going on. I could see the little people were busy scurrying about, going hither and thither on their horses and carts – more fetching and carrying, I supposed. I could feel some of them walking up and down my legs, then over my chest up to my neck. More fun and games for the children, I thought.

Not a bit of it. They had not come to play. They were pacing purposefully up my arm, down my leg, across my chest from shoulder to shoulder. They were stretching a thin ribbon from my waist to my shoulder, from my ankle to my waist, from my wrist to my shoulder. I was being measured!

They were measuring all of me, my head too, and even my feet – and that tickled me. They then made it clear they wanted me to lift my hips so that they could pass a ribbon underneath me and measure my waist.

With the measuring all done, they were suddenly all gone, and I was left alone on the beach with Gran Baruta and Tapit. The old lady came and sat on her rock nearby. From there, with Tapit beside her, she began to talk to me. The more she talked, the more I found I could understand at least something of what she was trying to tell me. When I didn't understand, when I looked too puzzled, Tapit would act out for me whatever she was trying to say.

I think she was trying to tell me how pleased she was I had come, and how like Gulliver I was – not as tall as he was but big enough – and that Gulliver had come to the island a long, long time ago, nearly three hundred years before, that her grandfather as a little boy had known him very well and liked him, how people on the island lived long lives, that she was 145 herself – if I understood the number right – and how Gulliver had taught English to her grandfather and everyone on the island so that now all the people on Lilliput could speak two languages, their own and Gulliver's language, which was English. Gulliver, she seemed to be telling me, had taught them all so much that they had not known or understood.

I was full of questions. So I tried then, using the little English I knew and some sign language and acting to help me, the question I had been longing most to ask. I held my arms out wide. 'Is this England? Fore Street? Am I . . . in England?'

They looked at one another, and then Tapit shook his head, and speaking slowly to help me understand, he said: 'Here, Son of Gulliver, you are on the island of Lilliput. This is Lilliput. England is far, far away, over the sea.'

He was pointing out to sea, at the horizon, at the sun going down. I understood well enough.

My heart sank. So this was not England, after all. I may have been welcomed like an old friend. These little people may have been the kindest people on Earth. But Mevagissey was not the village I had just seen down by the harbour. Uncle Said was not here. Mother would never be coming here. They were far away over the sea.

I wanted to be alone. I walked away from them along the beach, and lay down on the sand. I closed my eyes to stop my tears coming. But Mother would not leave my mind now.

All I could think of was that one day she would

arrive in England and find me not there, not with Uncle Said in his café on Fore Street, Mevagissey. It would break her heart, as it broke mine now, to think that between her and me there was a great wide ocean, full of waves and storms, and that I might never see her again.

I promised myself there and then as I lay on that beach, that some day I would cross the sea despite all the waves and storms, and find her.

SECOND
Part

CHAPTER NINE

Where Was I?

A small voice in my left ear was interrupting my story.

'You haven't told her about us,' it said. 'We were there. It's our story too, you know.'

Another voice spoke up, in my right ear this time. 'And working very hard to feed you, if you want to know, in case you've forgotten! All you did was sleep. You kept falling asleep.'

Then in my left ear again. 'You were snoring too in your sleep, loudly, like thunder.'

'I'm getting to you,' I told them. 'Just be patient. How can you be in the story if I haven't even met you yet? Now . . . where was I?'

'On the beach,' said J.J., ignoring both of them, and encouraging me to go on. 'The sun was going down,' she went on, 'and I really do want to hear the rest of the story. Tell me, tell me.'

So I told her.

I woke, wondering where I was. It was a while before I could gather my thoughts and my memory to make sense of where I was or what I was seeing. I sat up and looked about me.

The sea shore was crowded with little people, who were sitting there silently watching me wake up. I stretched and yawned and they all found that very funny. The old lady, sitting on her rock, was smiling up at me. The look on her face, and on all their faces, told me something was up.

Now that Gran Baruta saw I was awake, she stood up and, when she did, they all did. There was a buzz of excitement all about me. And then I saw why. They were presenting me with a suit of clothes: a shirt, a waistcoat, a long red coat with silver buttons, britches, a pair of buckled shoes and a three-cornered hat – all of which was very much how Tapit and all the men of Lilliput seemed to dress. It took at least six of these little people to hold up and show me just one of the shoes. The long red coat with the silver buttons took dozens of them. And all were smiling, proud of everything they had made for me.

I could not believe it. In a few hours of one day they had made all these clothes! And for me! I felt so honoured. I wanted to say something, to thank them, but I was deeply moved and could not speak. I was soon sitting there on the beach, the hat on my head, my lap and arms piled high with my new suit of clothes.

Clutching everything to me, I got to my feet. I wanted to try these wonderful clothes on at once, and I could see they were longing for me to do just that. But I didn't want to change in front of them. Gran Baruta saw at once what I was thinking, why I was hesitating, and began waving her stick at the dunes behind me. I turned and ran up the beach carrying

my clothes in a bundle, trying not to drop anything. I disappeared into the dunes, where I speedily transformed myself into a very well-dressed giant, a Lilliputian giant. The clothes all fitted perfectly, the shoes and the hat too.

When I reappeared to them, and stood at the top of the dune, arms raised in the air, they all broke into wild applause. Gran Baruta, I noticed, was overwhelmed at the sight of me. She may have looked stern sometimes, but I liked Gran Baruta. She laughed easily, and she cried easily. She never hid her feelings. As I was to learn, all Lilliputians were like that. They spoke with their hearts.

From that moment on, I was a fugitive no more, a refugee no more, a migrant no more, as I had been in the camp with Mother, as I had been on our long journey to the sea. I belonged somewhere now. I belonged here with these

wonderful people, who had welcomed me so warmly. They were my people. My place was with them. Lilliput was my home. I might not be small like them, but I was one of them, and they wanted me to stay, to be one of them. That was why they had welcomed me and fed me, why they had made me my new clothes.

I only wished that Mother was with me, that I didn't miss her so much. I was happy, but at the same time my heart was heavy with sadness.

Clothes were not all they gave me on that first day. Whilst some of them had been busying themselves cutting and shoemaking and hat-making, others had been creating another surprise for me, and there was just as much excitement about this as there had been about the presentation of the new clothes.

That same evening, with Gran Baruta and Tapit at my side, we walked right across the island to the farthest end, the mountainous end. Led by and followed by a huge throng of little people, with the children running and skipping ahead of us, we made our way through fields and tracks and came to the village, by the sea, by the harbour. The narrow streets were hardly wide enough for me to pass through. The houses were tiny, the whole place was tiny. No roof was higher than my knee. Then we came down to the harbour. Some of the fishing boats were tied up and others were at anchor out in the bay.

From there I could more clearly see the other island that I had noticed before. I bent down and tapped Gran Baruta on the shoulder and pointed it out.

'Blufescu,' she said.

But she told me no more, and nor did Tapit. I could see that neither of them wanted even to look at it. I felt even then that there was something about the island of Blufescu that made them nervous and uncomfortable, something that they did not want me to know about.

Wherever I was led around the island that evening, the people seemed to know I was coming. The welcome they gave me was overwhelming. They were throwing flowers from their windows.

They were clapping and cheering me in the streets. It looked as if everyone on the island had turned out to greet me, to watch me go by. Hundreds of them joined the procession, following us through the streets, past the houses around the harbour, a piping band of flutes and drums leading the way now, the children dancing on ahead, doing handstands and somersaults – they were wonderfully agile, these Lilliputian children, everyone an acrobat, it seemed to me.

We soon left the village and the harbour behind us, and followed the path down into a deep valley and along a stream where there were flowers growing everywhere on either side, beautiful flowers, magenta and purple, and orange too – there were marigolds everywhere. I was later to discover that marigolds especially grew in wild abundance all over the island.

Seeing the stream had made me thirsty again. I stopped to drink. The water was clear and sweet and cooling. But by stopping and crouching down to drink, it seemed I had encouraged some of the children to climb up on to me. And this was why, as soon as we were on our way again, I found myself with a dozen or more children clinging on to me, some peeking out of my pockets, others sitting on my shoulders. Lilliputian children, I was already discovering, especially loved to perch on my shoulders, on my hat too! I think they just like to ride as high as possible.

We came up out of the valley and walked through fields of sheep, and I saw beyond them steep hills, a wide plain below, with the high rocky mountain beyond. And then I saw, right up against the rock face under the mountain, the biggest building I had yet encountered on the island. It was made of wood – as were all the other buildings on Lilliput. For them it must have been huge, but for me it was little more than a small hut with a straw roof, and a door that was just about big enough and wide enough for me to crawl in. They were showing it to me with great pride. Evidently this was to be my house. They had made it for me, and like my suit of clothes, they had done it all in one day.

I stood there gazing at it, marvelling at it all. They were waiting for me to go in, waving me forward, welcoming me into my home. Little did they know how much this meant to me, to have a home again.

CHAPTER TEN

Thank You

I had to bend down a bit to go in through the door. Inside, against the far wall, was a bed, my bed. It stretched almost the length of my house, and was wide enough and long enough for me to be able to lie down easily. The ceiling was low, but I could stand upright, just. At one end was a fireplace and beside it a chair made of wood with a back and seat made of woven rushes, and beside that, under the window, a sturdy-looking table. There was a plate, a spoon, a cup all made in wood, and the right size for me. They had thought of everything.

I had supposed that some of the little people, and certainly Gran Baruta, would have followed me into the house. But once I was inside, I found myself all alone. I peered out through the window. They were all gathered outside, in silence. Then out of this silence came a humming, and I saw the children swaying to it and soon they all were, Gran Baruta too, and Tapit. It was a sound that warmed my heart. It was Mother's lullaby, my song. They were humming our song – my first indication of how quick they were to learn, these Lilliputians. I knew they wanted me to go out and join them, that they were hoping and expecting I would.

But I was in no hurry. I needed time to gather my thoughts. And anyway, I had to try out everything in the house. I sat in the chair. I stretched out on the straw mattress on the bed and looked up at the ceiling. They had painted a dark blue sky on it, with a yellow crescent moon and there were stars up there too. Lying on my bed I thanked those lucky stars. I thanked God, and I thanked Mother for making me get on that boat. Even if I never got to England, I thought, never got to see her again, this could be my home forever, I would be happy here, and safe.

But then I thought again. Mother would soon be in England, waiting for me in Fore Street, Mevagissey – she might be there already. I told myself I must always try to remember that, and must keep the promise I had made myself. One day I would go there and find her.

They were still humming out there, Mother's lullaby, the song they had now made their own. After a while, I got up off my bed and went to the door. When I opened it and appeared, they stopped humming, waiting for me to say something. I knew the words in English that I wanted to say to them.

'Thank you,' I said. 'Thank you.'

Later, lying in bed in my very own house, I made Mother another promise: that every night before I went to sleep I would speak to her, talk to her out loud as if she was sitting there on my bed. I told her that first night in my new home all about Lilliput and the kindness of the little people, about Gran Baruta and Tapit, and how good they all had been to me, about my clothes and my house, that I was safe and happy with them, and how I thought they spoke two languages, and one of them was English, which was lucky for me because I knew a little English from my cricket, and from Jimbo and the other aid workers at the camp, enough to say a word or two, and to understand enough.

I told her my new name, 'Son of Gulliver' – and how the children liked to call me Owzat – but that I would never forget my old name, nor Father, nor Hanan, nor her. I would always be Omar. And I would not forget my old home, nor our language – I spoke to her in Pashto of course. I told her how I hoped she would soon be safe and well with Uncle Said in Fore Street, Mevagissey, in England.

'Are you there already?' I asked her. 'You must talk to me, Mother, tell me. Then I'll know you are alive. Please talk to me.' But she did not.

So that was the end of my first day on Lilliput.

It had been a long day, but one I shall never forget.

CHAPTER ELEVEN

Zaya and Natoban

'You still have not told J.J. about me,' whispered the small voice in my left ear, Zaya's voice.

'Nor me,' said the other voice in my right ear, Natoban's voice, louder – he always spoke louder.

'I will, I will,' I said. 'You're going to be in the story any moment now, you'll see. Now, can I go on?'

I went on before they could stop me.

Without these two friends of mine, Zaya and Natoban, who you see now sitting on my shoulders, I said to J.J., I'm not sure I would ever have learnt to speak English properly. These two, along with Gran Baruta and Tapit, taught me well. I had no choice.

I had to learn it. No one in Lilliput spoke a word of Pashto, of my own language.

In the days and weeks that followed I learnt fast. Children make the best teachers. For a start they don't mind if you make mistakes. They are used to it. They don't think there is anything wrong with it. They know that making mistakes is how you learn. And Lilliputian children, like most children, are playful, and quick, so they make teaching and learning fun. They want it to be fun. And these two were eager that I should learn. They wanted me to understand them, and I wanted them to understand me. So with this kind of encouragement I learnt quite quickly and easily.

There was so much I still wanted to know, but could not ask, so much I wanted to tell them, and could not. I had no idea, for instance, in my early days on Lilliput, how old most of these Lilliputians – apart from Gran Baruta – might be. In time I learnt from the children how old each of them was. Counting on fingers helped with this. I knew four and six already of course, from cricket. So that was a start. I learnt my numbers in English before almost any other words.

They explained to me that, in Lilliput, children were children until they were thirty. They all found it very hard to believe when I told them that a giant like me was only twelve – which was my age, by the way, when I first arrived on Lilliput.

But now, J.J., the time has come for me to tell you about Zaya and Natoban, who, after four years of living on Lilliput, became my best friends in all the world. Zaya is sitting on my left shoulder, Natoban on my right. Zaya is thirty-three, Natoban thirty-three. So not children any more, but children when I first knew them. They are brother and sister, twins. Soon after I arrived on the island, Gran Baruta made them my guardians. It is something that was very common there. Everyone who was old or alone in this world had a young guardian or two to look after them. I wasn't old, but I was alone.

So I became their adopted brother, and they

became my adopted sister and brother. We adopted one another. Brothers and sisters for life, as you will see.

Now that they were in the story the two of them were much happier, punching the air in delight at every mention of their names.

. 'Brothers and sisters for life,' they echoed in my ears. 'Go on, Owzat, go on!'

So I did.

Zaya and Natoban came every day to my house with a dozen or so children helping them. They brought me all the food and drink I needed, and wood for the fire too. I soon realised that, with me being so huge, it took many hands and a lot of work to look after me. I loved having them with me. They would often sit on the window ledge beside my table and watch me eat. They always seemed amazed at all I did, at how much I was eating and drinking, what huge strides I took when I walked across the room, how loud it

was when I talked. If I ever tried to talk in a whisper, that just made them laugh. Lilliputian children, like all children, love life, and love to laugh. They can be cautious, but never fearful. They feel deeply and think deeply, which is why they speak their minds – and

often interrupt – and why they ask so many questions. They always have a lot to say, and that's because they care so much about everything and everyone. They say what they think, what they believe. They speak truth. Children do that.

And they are endlessly inquisitive too. These two loved to explore, and to explore me – especially in those early days, before I became familiar to them. If ever I sat down, they would climb up on to me. They were the ones who came to call me 'Mountain Man'. Soon I was Mountain Man or Owzat or Son of Gulliver to everyone on the island.

Lilliputians are wonderful climbers. Zaya and Natoban could always find a way up my coat and on to my shoulders. Out walking with them around the island, they always wanted a ride, didn't you? Other children would often join us and clamber all over me. Whenever there wasn't room for them on my shoulders because there were too many up there already, Zaya and Natoban would find their way down into my coat pockets, peer out from there, talk to me from there and be quite happy. In the end they travelled mostly in my pockets.

I must have become a strange sight in those early days, wandering the island with my two constant companions – and that's what they were to me. These two were always my guides on my travels around the island.

Natoban liked to sit as he is now, beside my right earlobe, tweaking it one way or the other to show me which way I should go, and pulling down on my lobe once whenever he wanted me to stop, and twice if he wanted me to sit down.

As we walked, Zaya would point out to me this and that and tell me what everything was called in English, and have me repeat it. And sometimes when she asked, I would tell her Pashto words – she can speak Pashto now just as well as I can speak English.

Soon, I came to think of them not just as friends, but as much more than that.

I had a new sister, and a brother too.

CHAPTER TWELVE

Dark Clouds

'And by the way, I can speak some Pashto words too,'
Natoban insisted.

'I can speak more,' Zaya said.

'That's only because you talk more anyway,' Natoban
told her.

'I don't.'

'You do.'

'Can I please go on?' I said.

'You go on, Omar,' J.J. said, impatient but laughing.
'I'm listening. I want to hear. I want to hear.'

Her boat lay still on the silent sea, almost as if she
too was waiting for me to go on.

*

All the time, I was discovering more and more of the life of the people on the island. Standing high on the mountain above my home I could see the whole of Lilliput spread out below me, the tracks spreading like a great web all over the island through the forests and fields, from house to farm.

The soaring eagles were no bigger than flies to me, the blowing whales at sea no larger than sardines, the sheep and cows and pigs were hardly the size of mice. Everywhere I looked the little people were out at work in the fields with their horses, and the fishing boats were ploughing through the waves on the open sea. There were always children out playing, or climbing the trees – and few of these trees were any taller than my hand. The children would be swimming in the sea or splashing in the streams. And they would often be singing as they played their games. They loved to sing, and I loved to hear them.

As I think I have told you, J.J., the island was very small. From my mountain top, I could see just about everything and everyone. I very soon got to know every farmhouse, every street in the village by the sea, every boat sailing in or out of the harbour. I could soon recognise all the people too, knew where they lived, what work they did. Zaya and Natoban took me everywhere, showed me everything, told me all about the island, made me feel at home.

In the village there was no school, as there had been in my town, or none that I could see. I learnt from Zaya and Natoban that on Lilliput everyone taught everyone, so there was no need for a school. They didn't even seem to know what a school was.

And they answered all my questions too – except one.

I wanted still to know about the island I could see across the channel from Lilliput, the one I knew was called Blufescu, the one no one seemed to want to talk about. More than once I tried asking these two. But they always looked the other way and would not say a word. Zaya shivered sometimes even at the mention of the name, and I noticed that when she did, Natoban would often take her hand in his to comfort her.

On clear days when there was no sea mist over the channel – as there often was between the two islands – I could see to the mountain on Blufescu, a high mountain with a jagged, pointed peak. It seemed to be a bigger and longer island than Lilliput, crescent-like in shape, the horns of the crescent pointing towards Lilliput, like the claws of an angry crab. Often I would see dark, threatening clouds hanging over Blufescu.

I wondered who lived there and why it was that the little people of Lilliput could scarcely bring themselves to look at the place, let alone talk about it.

It was true, it did not look a welcoming place to me at all. Every time I looked across the sea at the clouded island of Blufescu, I felt I had been very lucky to wash up on Lilliput.

And, as I would come to learn soon enough, I was right about that.

CHAPTER THIRTEEN

A Tree to Climb On

There seemed no end to the kindness and hospitality of these good people. I could not go into their tiny houses of course, but I was often invited to bend down and peer in through their windows, to see a newly born, or to wave at an old person sitting by a stove. I could scarcely pass by a house without being offered a loaf of freshly baked bread, which of course was hardly a mouthful to me.

Wherever I went, farming families were always proud to show me their animals; to them any animal – farm animal or wild animal – was treated like another member of the family. But the horses I met never liked me that much. They would toss their heads at me and show me the whites of their eyes. I was just too big for them. I would try lying down in a field to make myself as small as I could, and then I would reach out to them very slowly. But they were not stupid. They knew I was the same towering giant they had seen before. Many a time I tried to make friends with them, and many a time they would turn their backs on me and kick out. They had sharp little hooves, so a kick on my knuckles or ankles could really hurt.

The children, who seemed to follow me in droves wherever I went, always loved it when a horse kicked out at me. They loved it when they heard me crying out, or saw me shaking the pain off my knuckles, or hopping about. They would play with my words as if they were toys, and 'owzat' had become their favourite toy. In fact, that word was how most children always greeted me now on the island.

'Hello, Owzat! Good morning, Owzat.'

With everyone talking English to me, I learnt quickly enough how to understand it. Speaking it wasn't so easy. I had these two, usually sitting on my shoulders, just as they are now. Zaya and Natoban were always with me, always teaching me words, reminding me, correcting me, especially my accent.

'You speak it quite well now,' Zaya whispered in my left ear.

'Only quite well,' said Natoban. 'We speak it better. And by the way, I think you've gone on long enough with the story. Zaya and me, we do know it, you know.'

'J.J. wasn't there. She doesn't know it, does she?' I told him.

'I wish I had been,' J.J. said. 'I want to know everything, all of it.'

Natoban squeezed my earlobe – this was often how he showed his irritation or impatience. I ignored it, shook my head to stop him, and went on anyway.

The children on Lilliput especially liked it when I tried to speak. They would giggle and laugh at me, and tease me, but never cruelly. The people of Lilliput were never cruel, not to me, not to one another, not to the animals. It is not in their nature.

I often tried to imagine how I must have been to them, this strange visitor who towered above them, this giant they had taken in and looked after, with his big hands, big feet, big nose and big ears. I was a tree to climb on – the grown-ups were soon using me like this too. I once counted seventy Lilliputians climbing all over me at the same time. They would swing on me, walk along my outstretched arm, even balance on my head sometimes. If I lay down, they would dance on me, bounce up and down on me. They loved to mimic me, my accent, my loud voice, my huge steps. They walked like me, talked like me. And they soon discovered I was ticklish, that it didn't take much to make me break into giggles. They liked to hear me laugh, and I loved laughing too. I had not laughed like this, played like this, loved life like this since before the war came to my town and my world of home, and happiness had come to an end. When I laughed and played with my new friends in Lilliput,

I could forget all that. Laughing helps you to forget. Friends help you to forget.

Whatever I did, wherever I went, it was always with Zaya and Natoban. They were and they are my guardians and my guides – even if they do interrupt me sometimes, and pinch my earlobes. We roamed the island together, climbed the mountain together – easy for me, not so easy for them. They tried to teach me to swim – everyone on Lilliput seemed as happy and natural in the water as out of it, but I could never do it. I never trusted the water to hold me up.

I had never lived by the sea, and I think I had seen too many people drowning in it. Thanks to these two, it wasn't long before I knew the island from end to end, before it became like a home to me. And every evening when they took me back to my house, there was food and drink waiting for me on my table, and a fire burning to warm the house.

Sometimes Gran Baruta and Tapit would be waiting there by the fire. I never ate alone, never felt alone – they made sure of that. I would show off to them words I had learnt that day, and this, I could see, pleased them both. During these evenings and over the many months and years I lived on Lilliput, she and Tapit were my most frequent visitors, and I came to know them well and trust them. They were my new family now, Tapit my uncle, Gran Baruta my grandmother, and these two, like brother and sister to me.

I felt I could tell them everything – who I was, where I had come from, about the war in my country, and how it had destroyed our lives, and driven Mother and me and millions like us from our homes, and forced us to find safety in other countries.

The more English I learnt to speak, the more I could tell them, and the better I could understand what they told me. I remember how, as I was describing the bombing of my town, telling them how Father had been killed, how Hanan had disappeared, Gran Baruta reached out and held my little finger tight.

'Gulliver always said,' she told me, 'that this was why we all had to learn to be kind to one another in this life, that fear and suspicion and anger and greed and hate always lead to war, and that one war always leads to another, sooner or later, that in his world – and his world was the same world you come from, Son of Gulliver – there was always war, that it is a disease that would destroy everyone. The only cure for it, he told us, is goodwill, and kindness and understanding. That's why we have become as we are, here on Lilliput. It is because of Gulliver, because of what he told us of your world. He was warning us.'

Between Gran Baruta and Tapit – and my friends sitting here on my shoulders – I was discovering so much about Gulliver: for instance, how he had brought the English language to Lilliput three hundred or more years before, which was why everyone on the island now spoke two languages, Lilliputian and English. I discovered, in time, that the suit of clothes I was wearing had not been newly made for me, as I had always supposed, but was altered from some of Gulliver's clothes that they had kept and looked after when he left. As for my house, it had been Gulliver's house when he was on Lilliput. Like my clothes, it had been cared for all these years, and looked after, so that everything would be ready for him if he ever came back.

'He never did come back,' Gran Baruta told me sadly one evening. 'But we never forgot him, never forgot what he did for us, how his wise words changed our life here forever, helped us become who we are. The spirit of Gulliver lives on. He may not have come back as we had hoped, but you did, Son of Gulliver, you did.'

So I was learning more and more about this Gulliver

who had been there before me. But about Blufescu, they would tell me nothing. Just a mention of it and everyone fell silent. Blufescu was a closed book.

CHAPTER FOURTEEN

Talking to Mother

At night-times especially, my head was full of all that was happening to me, all I was discovering every day, all Baruta was telling me. I was never sure I had understood everything properly, but I did realise soon enough that my arrival on Lilliput was the most important and most welcome event ever since the coming of Gulliver, my father, my predecessor. I would tell Mother more about it every night, and it was not easy to explain. But I loved talking to her, and it was a relief to speak Pashto, speak my own language again. In Pashto I could say exactly what I meant.

I was sure Mother must have arrived safely in England by now. I would often ask her about how it was in Fore Street, Mevagissey, and in Uncle Said's café. I longed for her to answer, but she never did of course. I tried to reassure her that I was well looked after and safe and happy. I told her more every evening about Lilliput – and about this Gulliver man who had come here a long time ago from England. I told her that I was speaking English really well now, much better than I ever had in the refugee camp with Jimbo and the other aid workers. I told her how good I thought this was, because when I came to England I would be able to speak in English as well as English people do. I told her how strange it was not to be called Tiny any more, that in Lilliput I was a giant, and how I loved being a giant, and how much I missed her, and all my friends at home, and how I longed to play cricket with them, but that I knew I never would, that those days were over, and how that made me very sad. I poured all my thoughts out to her, all my hopes.

It was as I was talking to her one night that I had

a sudden and a wonderful idea. I told Mother all about it. Tapit might help. I knew he was a boatbuilder, a carpenter, that he was practical, good at making things – Gran Baruta was always telling me this. She was very proud of him. She had taken me down to the harbour once and had shown me one of the fishing boats he had made – his pride and joy, and hers too, I could tell. I would do it, I told Mother. I would start tomorrow.

The next day I went down to the beach where we used to pick up most of the driftwood for the fire, and found a few small pieces of wood just about the right size and shape for what I had in mind. I came back and told Tapit everything I would need, and explained as best I could in my excited English what the game of cricket was, all the rules and how it was played. He looked at me rather blankly I remember. I said I would need several wooden bats, two sets of stumps also from wood, and two leather balls in case one got lost. I drew everything for him on a piece of paper, showed him how big, or how small, everything had to be.

A few weeks later, I had a lot more to tell Mother, and I knew how much she would love to hear it. She knew how much I loved cricket. I could tell her now that I was teaching the Lilliputian children the wonderful game of cricket, and they were loving it already, and how brilliant they were at playing it. I explained to her there was a flat field just outside the village that made a perfect pitch.

We had to share it with the sheep, but that didn't matter. We had twenty-two players – as we should – and several bats made of wood by Tapit, and two leather balls made by his cousin who was the tanner in the village, all just the right size for Lilliputians. We had all we needed. It took a while for me to explain the rules, and to teach them how to play. Not everyone liked it, of course, but most did. And those that didn't just thought it was funny.

'It is funny,' Zaya said. 'And it takes a long time and it's also boring and anyway I still don't understand the rules. And when the ball hits you, it hurts.'

Natoban shushed her and I went on.

I told Mother how they shouted 'Owzat!' to start with at every ball they bowled. Sometimes the whole island was there to watch, cheering every ball, every catch, every run, every 'Owzat!' I told Mother it was just like being at home in Afghanistan, except that in Lilliput the pitch was grassy and flatter, and there were not nearly so many stones. Of course the players were rather small, which meant I couldn't play. So I had to be the coach as well as the umpire.

I told Mother a lot about cricket because I knew it would make her smile, how the Lilliputians were natural cricketers, that they had sharp eyes, and quick reactions, and their timing was perfect. The Lilliputian children hit the ball hard, bowled it fast, and they could run like the wind between the wickets out in the field. Before long the children were teaching their mothers and fathers. Everyone on Lilliput seemed to want to try the new game.

'Not me,' said Zaya, pulling on my earlobe. 'Not me. I like running, and riding horses, and swimming and climbing. And by the way, Owzat, I love telling stories too, remember?' She had climbed down off my shoulder by now, and was standing on my open hand, hands on her hips looking up at me, a determined look on her face. 'Owzat, I want to tell the next part of the story. Gran Baruta says I tell stories really well.'

'All right,' I said. 'But first let me explain to J.J. about the apple tree.'

'What about the apple tree?' said J.J. 'What's that got to do with cricket anyway?'

'I'll tell you,' I said. 'It is the most famous tree on the island.'

It had been planted from old, old seeds – seeds passed on from tree to tree from an apple that had been found in Gulliver's pocket three hundred years before.

So this was called Gulliver's Tree. It was my first spring on Lilliput and all over the island there was great excitement. Everyone was waiting for the first blossom to show on the apple tree, Zaya told me.

Then someone spotted it. I remember we were all out on the field playing a game of cricket when Gran Baruta appeared with Tapit at her side. At once the game was abandoned and we followed them to the

famous tree and sat down all around it. Everyone seemed to know what was going to happen, except me. And no one would tell me.

I was sitting there with these two on my shoulders, and a dozen other children perched on me, all of us

waiting in silence. Then Baruta pointed up to the blossom on the tree and said, 'Now I can begin the story.'

This story explained so much I had not yet understood. I could see from the faces all around me that it meant so much to every single person on Lilliput. Everyone was there. No one ever missed Baruta's talk of the coming of Gulliver.

As soon as she began, I felt she was telling it just to me, and that I was the only one there. I knew everyone else felt the same way. This was the story of Gulliver, and of Lilliput and Blufescu. It was to be my story now too.

I looked down at Zaya, still waiting there on my hand.

'All right,' I said, 'your turn now.'

Zaya climbed up on to my shoulders. 'I'll start then, shall I?' she said.

And she did.

THIRD
Part

CHAPTER FIFTEEN

Round End Good. Sharp End Bad

Once a year on Lilliput, on Gulliver's Day, which is the first day the apple tree blossoms, we all gather under the tree to listen to Gran Baruta telling us about the coming of Gulliver.

'Listen and hear, dear ones, dear Lilliputians, and believe and never forget.' That's how Gran Baruta always began the story. 'It is hard to believe, but there was a time when we on this island were a very different people.'

It was over three hundred years ago – Gran Baruta's own grandfather was a boy at the time – and Lilliput was a very different place. We had an emperor then who lived in a grand palace, which has now become our meeting hall in the village. The emperor of Lilliput surrounded himself with nobles and friends and advisors who lived only to please him and serve him and to become richer. Outside the palace, in the countryside, the people worked the fields every day of the year, every day of their lives, whatever the weather. They also lived only to please him and serve him, but they remained poor. There was one life of leisure and plenty for the emperor and his court and his friends, another life of endless labour and poverty for everyone else.

The emperor was an arrogant man, greedy and foolish, and wanted only to remain rich and remain emperor. He did not care about his people. From them he expected only obedience and work. And work they did, every hour of every day to feed the emperor and his court, to provide them with all they needed. Anyone who disobeyed him he would banish to the island of Blufescu across the

sea. The emperor's opinion was the law, and if you disobeyed the law then off you went to Blufescu, you and your family for life. So, of course, the people for the most part did as they were told, although not all of them, as you shall see.

It was the custom on Lilliput in those days to always eat a boiled egg for breakfast. On a whim one morning, the emperor decided to make a law. Because he had always opened his boiled egg at the round end, he decreed that everyone should do the same. 'Round end good. Sharp end bad.' That was his edict. From that day on, if you opened your boiled egg at the sharp end, it would be a crime, the act of a traitor, an act of grave disloyalty and disobedience to the emperor. The punishment, banishment to the island of Blufescu.

In time, Blufescu became an island full of banished people who only opened their eggs at the sharp end. So the people of the two islands became enemies, deadly enemies. They opened their eggs differently at breakfast and that was enough for them both to start a war. And as always happens, one war leads to another war. Each island built a fleet of great warships, and were making plans to invade one another. Any stranger arriving on the shores of either island was immediately thought of as an enemy or a spy, and imprisoned, or put to death.

One morning, as they were collecting shells along the shores of Lilliput, some children discovered, quite by chance, a great giant lying on the beach. At first they thought he must be dead. But when they came closer, they found that he was still breathing. They ran at once to the village to raise the alarm. Soon the emperor and his nobles, and his soldiers and all the people from all over the island were hurrying down to the shore. They were terrified at the sight of this great giant. 'A treacherous spy sent over from Blufescu!' cried the emperor. 'If he wakes up, he would kill us all. Look at the size of him! We must tie him down, anchor him firmly to the ground. Then he will be at our mercy, and we can do with him what we please.'

Whilst many of the Lilliputians ran back to fetch all the stakes and all the ropes they could find, the emperor's soldiers were ordered to approach the giant and fire hundreds of arrows into him as he slept, and these arrows had poisoned tips that would make the giant sleep long and deep.

'He may be more use to us alive,' the emperor said. 'Shoot all your arrows, so he will not wake up until we are ready. We must make him helpless.' So the emperor's soldiers did as they were told

and fired their poison arrows into the sleeping giant. He did not wake up for hours and hours.

When he did wake he found he could not move, that he was firmly tied down, by his hair, by his arms and legs. He struggled and he kicked but he could not move. Still only half awake, he told them that he meant no harm, that he was a sailor

called Gulliver, that his ship had been wrecked in a terrible storm. He begged them to untie him, to set him free. He promised he would do no harm to them. Of course, Gulliver spoke in English, so none of the Lilliputians could understand a word he said. And anyway, the emperor had no intention of releasing him. He ordered his archers to shoot more arrows into him to make him go back into a deep sleep.

They made a long low cart on wheels. Then, using every horse on the island, they hauled Gulliver into the courtyard of the palace. They forged great chains, and whilst he was still asleep they chained him up, so that when he woke Gulliver found he could sit up, and stand up, but he could walk only a few steps. He was the emperor's prisoner. Day and night, the soldiers stood around him guarding him, ready to shoot their poison arrows at this 'mountain man' as they called him, in case he tried to break from his chains.

Of course he was not at all pleased to be chained up, this mountain man, but otherwise he was quite happy. He was kept in the courtyard of the palace, and given all the food and drink he needed. He was the most famous person on the island, far more famous even than the emperor, which the emperor did not like. The Lilliputians crowded the courtyard every day to wonder at him. They brought gifts for him, fish, cheese, fruit, and they showered him with flowers. And Gulliver liked this. He liked these people. He did not like the emperor any more than the emperor liked him, but he saw there was great kindness in these people, and he was kind in return.

Meanwhile, the emperor and his nobles and advisors were deciding what they should do with this giant of a man. One said he should be killed at once, that it was too dangerous to keep him alive, that he was eating too much of the island's food, and that anyway he deserved to die because he was a spy sent from Blufescu, and it would teach people over there a lesson. Another said he was too big to kill. How could it be done? What would they do with the body? It would lie and rot in the sun and make a terrible smell. The emperor said nothing. He was thinking.

'No, no,' he said at last. 'I have a much better plan altogether. I have been watching this Gulliver. He likes it here. He likes our food, likes our people, and they like him. So we look after him, make him feel at home, and then when the time is right we will use him. He will help us defeat those traitorous sharp-end egg-eaters in Blufescu.'

'But how will you do this, O High and Mighty Emperor?' they cried.

'You will see,' said the cunning emperor, tapping his nose conspiratorially.

CHAPTER SIXTEEN

The Wrecking of the Warships

So the emperor went to see Gulliver, who was still chained up in the courtyard of the palace. 'I have decided the time has come, Mountain Man,' he said, 'to set you free from your chains. We have all come to trust you as a friend. We know now you will not harm us. We have fed you and sheltered you all this time, and the people of Lilliput have come to love you. I too have come to love you as a brother. So I shall set you free. No more chains. But I wonder, Gulliver, if you could help us in return. I am your friend, and I want you to be my friend, my best friend. In return for your help, you will not only be free, but you will live like an emperor. I will build you a great palace, you will be as rich as I am.'

Gulliver of course did not believe any of this. He came from England, a country where there was a king who ruled over the people, a king who was rather like this emperor. He knew better than to put his trust in the rich and powerful, in emperors or kings.

But of course he did want to be free of his chains. 'What exactly is it that you want me to do?' Gulliver asked the emperor.

'Those traitorous sharp-end egg-eaters across the sea in Blufescu,' the emperor began, 'we have heard they are preparing to attack us. They have a huge fleet of warships in the harbour, every one of them armed with many cannons. They are making ready to invade us. Somehow we have to stop them, Gulliver. You are the only one who can save us. I want you to sink their ships for us, all of them. Then Lilliput and its people, who have been so good and kind to you, we will be safe forever.'

As Gulliver listened to all of this, he was looking around him at all the faces of the Lilliputians who were waiting for his reply.

'Very well, I will do my best to make you all safe,' he said, choosing his words very carefully. 'I shall see what I can do.'

The people cheered and cheered, and the emperor thanked him profusely. Then they released Gulliver from his chains, and set him free.

'I will need all the rope you have,' he told the emperor.

So all the rope on Lilliput was gathered and brought to him. He looped it around himself, and made ready. Gulliver kept his promise that day, but not quite in the way the emperor or anyone else was expecting. He did in a way that changed Lilliput and Blufescu forever.

With everyone on the island looking on, Gulliver waded out into the sea, past all the warships of the Lilliputian fleet lying at anchor in the harbour, and out into the waves of the open ocean beyond. At one point, halfway across, the sea in the channel was so deep that he had to swim. The current was not that strong, and it was not too far across, not for Gulliver, who could swim well. Soon enough he found he could walk again, easily enough, and was wading into the harbour on Blufescu.

There were warships all around him in the harbour, dozens of them, fifty cannons on every ship, all of them firing at him. But to Gulliver the cannon balls were no bigger than peas. They bounced off him – he could hardly feel them. From the shore all around they were firing their arrows at him, but hardly one of them ever reached him. By this time all the sailors, terrified at the sight of this approaching giant, jumped into the sea and were swimming for their lives for the shore.

Towering over the harbour now like a colossus, Gulliver reached down, and using the rope he had brought with him, he tied together all the anchor chains of the warships in the harbour. Then he turned, and wading out of the harbour, he began to haul them behind him, out towards the open ocean.

Once far enough out, he undid the ropes, and then, one by one, he gave each a mighty push and sent every one of those ships far out to sea. The emperor and all the people of Blufescu stood and watched in horrified silence as their great and proud fleet of warships drifted away, at the mercy now of wind and waves, to be wrecked on the rocks before their eyes. All this time the emperor and people of Lilliput were cheering from their rooftops, from the harbour wall, from all their warships in the harbour, as they witnessed this great triumph over their hated enemy.

But their cheering was soon to be silenced, when they saw what Gulliver was doing next. At first they thought he was simply wading and swimming back to Lilliput after his great victory, and the closer he came to the harbour, the more they cheered him. It took a while before they began to realise Gulliver was up to something else.

Tying his rope to the anchor chains of all the Lilliputian warships in the harbour, he was doing exactly as he had done to the warships in Blufescu. He was towing the great Lilliputian navy out to sea, in just the same way. All the sailors were

diving off the ships and swimming for the shore. The emperor and the people of Lilliput looked on in despair, as all their ships drifted away on to the rocks and were wrecked, just like the warships of Blufescu. Neither side had a single warship left afloat.

CHAPTER SEVENTEEN

The Eggy Part

*B*ut that wasn't the end of the story. Now comes the important part, the part Gran Baruta always liked telling best, the part all the children always liked best too. The 'eggy part', as Gran Baruta called it. 'As you all know, dear Lilliputians,' she would say, 'without Gulliver we should not be as we are today, living together in peace and friendship, living for one another, free to speak our minds, a free people, a happy people, mostly.'

That day, over three hundred years ago now, when he had sunk all the warships of Lilliput and Blufescu, Gulliver realised that was not good enough, that there was more that had to

be done. He knew that one side or the other –
or both – could always build more warships,
more weapons of war. He understood that to
make peace, it wasn't enough just to sink the
warships of both sides. He knew that to be sure
peace would last, all weapons of war had to be
destroyed.

So he made both emperors agree to surrender
every bow and arrow, every spear, every sword,
every musket, cannon and cannon ball. Gran
Baruta's grandfather was there, as a little boy –
she often reminded us of this as she was telling
her story. He saw it all, heard it all, remembered it
all – everything Gulliver did, every word he said,
how Gulliver built a raft and
loaded it again and again
with every weapon of war
from both islands, then

towed it far out to sea, where he tipped the raft upside down, and all their weapons of war ended up at the bottom of the ocean. 'That's where they belong. No weapons, no war,' Gulliver told them.

With the weapons gone, Gulliver now invited the emperor of Lilliput and the emperor of Blufescu, and all their people, to come to a great gathering on Lilliput, to talk about making peace, and about eggs.

The gathering took place outside Gulliver's house, under the mountain. All the Lilliputians sat together on one side of him, all the Blufescuans on the other. They would not speak to one another. They would not even look at one another. Gulliver sat on a chair outside his home, with a scowling emperor on either side of him. When Gulliver got up and began to speak, they both looked down at their nails or up at the sky, and pretended not to be listening, but they were.

'I come from a country, a world,' Gulliver told them – and he spoke their language well enough by now – 'where there is always a war somewhere, sometimes a dozen or more at a time. Often these wars are about God, or about how you say your prayers, or how you dress, or what you eat, or the language you speak, and some are about who owns the fish in the sea or the water in the wells. Sometimes they are ridiculous family squabbles between kings and emperors, about who owns this bit of land or that, this mountain or that, this island or that. Some kings and emperors are never happy unless they rule the world. So they make huge weapons of war, gather great armies, build warships by the hundreds. And they make war. And what happens?

'I shall tell you. Thousands upon thousands die. Houses and villages and towns are burnt to the ground. Children become orphans, wives become widows. There is starvation and misery and sorrow. Driven from their homes, people wander the world searching for safety and peace, and are strangers wherever they go. They are people without a home.

But there can be no peace in such a world. And at the end of any war, is anything resolved? For a time it might seem so maybe. But the trouble is that win or lose, sooner or later, one war only begins another war. This is how it is in the world I come from,' Gulliver told them, 'and how it will always be until all wars everywhere are ended for good. And sadly, in my world, there is little sign of that.

'I have lived here amongst the Lilliputians long enough to know that once upon a time, and for hundreds of years, the people on this island and the people on Blufescu were friends. You all know the story well enough, how one day the emperor of Lilliput, who was all powerful and made quite mad by his power, made a decree, a law, that in future all boiled eggs had to be eaten round end first, and that anyone who eats their eggs sharp end first should be considered a traitor and henceforth be banished forever to the island of Blufescu.

'Of course there were those who objected to this, who refused to eat their boiled eggs round end first, and the emperor banished them. These "traitors", so-called, these sharp-end egg-eaters, all ended up on Blufescu, and those loyal to the emperor, all the round-end egg-eaters, remained on Lilliput. So, all because of eggs, the two islands soon became sworn enemies, each insisting theirs was the only right and proper way to eat eggs. That was how the egg war began.

'Fishing boats were turned into warships. Ploughs were turned into swords and spears and cannon. Both islands armed themselves to the teeth with weapons. Each side built up a huge army of horsemen and swordsmen and lancers and archers. Fear and suspicion and hate ruled on both islands. Each threatened to invade the other. Each built walls to fortify their island against enemies.

'Oh, you foolish people,' Gulliver told them all. 'You are as foolish as my people back at home in England, in Europe. You, us, we are all led by kings and emperors and governments into wars we don't want. We are led to make strangers of friends, the enemies of friends. At home in England, I went to war once myself. I have seen what was done with my own eyes. Wars make monsters of us all. On my return from the wars I tried to speak up against it. They would not listen. They hounded me out. I became a stranger in my own land. But here, amongst friends, I can try. Here I am big, I am a giant. I could destroy you all. But I am not a mad giant. I am a gentle giant mostly – you know that. And I am angered only by silly greedy people who fight wars about how to eat eggs. I will show you now, right away, how we can all stop all this nonsense. Do not go away.'

CHAPTER EIGHTEEN

How to Crack an Egg, Peacefully

Gulliver got up from his chair, and disappeared inside his house. He was back in a moment holding an egg in one hand and a small bowl in the other. 'From now on, this is what we shall do, you, me, all of us,' he declared. 'From now on not one of us will crack open an egg at the sharp end, nor at the round end. We shall crack open our eggs only in the middle, like this.'

And with that, Gulliver tapped the egg smartly on the side of the bowl, cracking it open in the middle. 'This way we can have scrambled eggs, fried eggs or poached eggs, we can even make

an omelette. This way we all open our eggs the same way. This way neither side wins and neither side loses. This way we will all be friends again, and there will be no more war between us. There will be no need for war, and no need for weapons. Soon it won't matter how we eat our eggs, because we shall all be friends, and then we can laugh together about how absurd and sad and silly and unbelievable it was that we ever had an egg war at all. This way Lilliputians and Blufescuans can be friends forever. What do you think? Are we all agreed?'

The emperors hung their heads in shame, as did everyone from both the warring islands.

'And no more warships? Agreed?' Gulliver said, wagging his finger. 'And no more bows and arrows, no more cannons or gunpowder or spears or swords. Agreed?'

'We agree,' replied both the emperors, and they spoke in unison.

'And now,' Gulliver told them, 'I would like

everyone here to stand up. I want you all to go and find someone from the other island, and shake hands, and do it looking one another in the eye, so that you mean it, so that each knows the other means it, means to be friends. Emperors first.'

So the emperors did as he said, and then all the people followed by his example. Maybe not all the people shook hands willingly that first time, but they did it. It was a start.

Gran Baruta told us that was the beginning of a peace which lasted throughout her grandfather's long life, and all through hers too. So since then, and thanks to Gulliver, Lilliput and Blufescu have had over three hundred years of peace.

On both our islands, we all learnt that kindness and understanding were the way forward, kindness towards one another, understanding between the two islands. Without that understanding, there can be no kindness; without that kindness, there can be no understanding. Gulliver told us this. Think of a stranger, an enemy as your friend, he said, and he will be your friend. It's quite simple. Think of your friend as your enemy and, sooner or later, you will end up fighting him. And let no emperor or king or government ever do your thinking for you. And treat any stranger coming to these shores as your friend. Be the people you wish to be, let no one decide for you. Guard your freedoms, guard your rights. Cling to them as to life itself!

And that is why, for hundreds of years on Lilliput and on Blufescu, we have never had an emperor or a king or government. We have no need of them. We decide everything amongst ourselves, don't we? We live for each other, look after each other, work for each other, teach each other, for the good and happiness of us all.

Everyone always clapped then, and echoed Gran Baruta's last words of her story. 'For the good and happiness of us all.'

Once he had made this peace, Gulliver stayed with us and lived amongst us for many more years, and during this time Lilliputians and Blufescuans lived always at peace with one another, trading freely, coming and going to one another's island as they pleased, some marrying one another and having children. And all of us, on both our islands, cracked our eggs in the middle and ate them fried, or poached or scrambled.

All this time Gulliver was teaching us his English language. He had learnt our language, now known as Lillifescuan, so he thought we should learn his. He was always saying that knowing the language of others is so important to the understanding of others, and that with understanding comes peace. So in time the people of both islands learnt to speak English, and of course we still do.

But then came the sad, sad day when Gulliver announced that as much as he had loved living amongst us, the time had come for him to go home to his family in England, that he missed them more and more every day. And despite everything, all the wars and suffering back home, he longed for his country, that it was where he belonged.

Gran Baruta's grandfather was one of those who helped build his boat. It took several months and hundreds of people from both islands to cut down the trees and build a boat big enough and strong enough to carry him safely over the seas back home to England. They had to make all the ropes and sails, and then fill the boat with all the food and water he would need for his long and arduous journey.

On the day Gulliver left, Gran Baruta told us how everyone gathered on the shore to say goodbye to him and to wish him a safe journey. The people from Blufescu had come over to see him off as well. They knew as well as we did how much Gulliver had done for us all. He had ended a war, made peace and taught us kindness. Standing in his boat, his sails set, Gulliver spoke to everyone on the shore. These were his last words to us, words Gran Baruta's grandfather never forgot.

'I promise I shall try to come back one day, my friends. That much I can promise you. If I do not, then it will only be because I cannot. And then maybe one day my son will come instead of me. I shall tell him all about you, I shall tell the world about you. Keep the peace. Be free, be happy.'

Gran Baruta reminded us often of those words. And she told us that even when they could no longer see the sail of Gulliver's boat on the horizon, they still stood there on the beach, all of them, arm in arm, Lilliputians and Blufescuans, until the sun sank into the sea.

And in a way Gulliver did keep his promise. He never did come back, but his son did, Owzat did. Owzat, Son of Gulliver, came just when we needed him. But that's his story to tell.

FOURTH
Part

CHAPTER NINETEEN

Blufescu

'So it's your turn again, Owzat,' said Zaya. 'You should tell J.J. all about Blufescu. About what happened. You should be the one to tell her, because you were the one who did it.'

To be honest, I thought this whole story had gone on quite long enough by now. But J.J. had been sitting there, leaning forward throughout it all, her eyes never leaving us, agog at our tale – whichever of us was telling it – and I could see she was longing to hear more.

'Blufescu,' she said. 'Come on, Omar, tell me about Blufescu. What happened? What did you do? Don't stop now.'

'All right,' I said, wondering how best to start. It was strange. This was my story and should have been easy to tell, but it wasn't. It was a while before I could find a way to begin.

The first time I ever heard Gran Baruta tell the Gulliver story was on my first Gulliver Day, in my very early days on Lilliput. All through the telling of the story, I was becoming more and more troubled. At first I wasn't quite sure what it was that was upsetting me. But then it came to me. I think I told you that I had noticed before quite often – and especially with Natoban and Zaya – that whenever I asked about the island of Blufescu, it always provoked a reaction that I had never really understood. It was only when I heard Gran Baruta telling Gulliver's story for the first time that I knew for sure that, for everyone on Lilliput, it was as if some fearful shadow hung over the island of Blufescu.

At every mention of Blufescu in Gran Baruta's story, I had noticed how everyone about me had become suddenly unsettled, troubled – as if they were hearing the rumble of distant thunder. It was clear to me now that all was far from well between the people of Lilliput and their neighbours across the sea on Blufescu. I had never liked to ask. Lilliputians were kind people, but private too. They would tell me when they were ready, I thought. But I had known for some time that something was wrong.

That night in my house, after hearing the story of the coming of Gulliver for the first time, I told Mother all about Gulliver, and about how much I liked being called his son. I did say – so that I would not upset her – how I hoped Father would not mind too much that I had another father now, in a way. As time passed I spoke to her less and less in Pashto, and much more in English because I thought it would be good practice, and because I imagined she had been in England for quite a while now and would understand me easily enough.

Every time I spoke to Mother I promised her again I would come to find her there in England, in Fore

Street, Mevagissey. Somehow I would find a way. It was strange, but it seemed easier for me to speak the truth to Mother, to tell her how I was feeling, now that she was not with me. The distance between us seemed in a way to bring us closer. I would come one day, I would – I promised her this – but I did tell her also how difficult it would be to leave a place where there was peace, and safety, where there was always enough food and drink, where I was not a stranger nor a refugee, where I had good friends, who were like family to me, and kind, and where I was big, a boy giant, where I was needed.

And Mother was the only one I felt I could confide in about the island of Blufescu, about how anxious everyone on Lilliput seemed to be about the place, and how puzzled I was. I told her how Gran Baruta had said how happy everyone was that I had come, that Son of Gulliver was 'needed', how I thought it must be something to do with Blufescu, but had no idea what it could be.

Standing high on the mountain above my house,

I would often look out across the sea towards Blufescu and wonder what was going on over there that seemed to alarm the Lilliputians as it did. There was so much I did not know, that I wanted to ask. Gran Baruta's story had explained all about Gulliver, and his coming, but there was so much I did not understand about Lilliput and Blufescu, about how these little people really saw me, and why I was 'needed'.

After that day when I first heard the story of Gulliver under the apple tree, I thought of asking Gran Baruta about Blufescu; but kind though she had been to me, I was always a little nervous of her. Tapit was constantly at her side, so Gran Baruta and I were never alone, and Tapit, I could tell, was wary of me, and very protective of her. Gran Baruta to me was like my grandmother had been at home in Afghanistan, the most important person in our family. Gran Baruta was the most important person on Lilliput, a figure of great wisdom and age and authority, who commanded universal respect. I just didn't like to ask her in case I upset her.

In the end I asked Zaya and Natoban straight out, didn't I? The three of us were all there together, I remember, scouring the beach for driftwood, for my fire. That was when they told me.

CHAPTER TWENTY

Bronar the Tyrant

'And I remember too.' Natoban was interrupting me. 'I'll explain,' he went on. 'We didn't want to tell Owzat, because we just didn't want to talk about Blufescu. Everyone on Lilliput was fearful of Blufescu, about Blufescu. Zaya and me more than anyone perhaps. We had good reason. But Gran Baruta had told us also that it was best not to talk about Blufescu, to try not to think about what was going on there. We had to think and speak of them as our friends, she said, whatever we might think, or they would soon become our enemies. Gran Baruta thought, as we all did, that everyone on Blufescu would know that we had a giant living with us on Lilliput, a friend. They had their telescopes and their spies. They could hardly miss Owzat, could they?

'Gran Baruta never said anything, but I know she hoped, as we all did on Lilliput, that they would not dare attack us. They knew Owzat was a man mountain, a huge giant with great strength and power, that all their muskets and spears and swords could not harm him. While Owzat was with us on Lilliput we were safe. Meanwhile, we just tried to forget that Blufescu was there, put the place out of our minds.

'For Zaya and me, though, that was never easy. I will tell you why.'

You might be thinking that after Gulliver there was a lasting peace between Lilliput and Blufescu, that we were all good friends. Well, once we were. For hundreds of years, we had lived as the best of friends. But then, about ten years ago, everything changed. And it was quite sudden. Until we talked on the beach that day, we had never told you that, like many of us living now on Lilliput, Zaya and I came from Blufescu. We were born there, grew up there, so we saw it happen all around us. We still don't like to talk about it.

It was one man, just an ordinary man, but he became a tyrant. Bronar, he was called. He was a boatbuilder, and a good boatbuilder too. Nobody on Blufescu built boats as fine and fast nor as strong as his. He made money, became rich, and then richer still, and soon he was the most powerful man on the island. Gran Baruta always said he must have been blinded by the glitter of gold, by a lust for power. He built himself a grand palace in the middle of the island. But a palace wasn't enough for him. He wanted to be emperor, to own the whole island and everyone that lived there. Mother and Father, Zaya and me, our whole family, we were soon to become his slaves.

Father died from overwork, Mother soon after, of a broken heart. And because they died we were told we had to leave our farm, that we had no right to stay in our house any more. We had nowhere to go. We lived in the fields, in the ditches, in the forests. We were starving. The emperor Bronar was always making new laws. Whenever we saw him coming, we had to lie down and kiss the ground at his feet. No one was allowed to leave the island, except the fishermen, and they had to give almost everything they caught to him. Everything on Blufescu belonged to Bronar. And no one was ever allowed to speak English again. Only Blufescuan. He created his own flag, a picture of

himself silhouetted in gold on a scarlet background, his fist raised. We all had to stand there as the trumpets sounded, and the flag of Blufescu was raised over the palace every morning. And we all had to chant: 'Blufescu forever! Blufescu first! Blufescu is best!'

We longed only to find a boat to escape over the sea to Lilliput, but many had tried and many had died, or been caught and beaten and imprisoned by Bronar's soldiers. Bronar's warships patrolled the coast to stop us from escaping. He built a high wall all the way round the shore. Our island became our prison. We weren't allowed even to speak the name of Lilliput. Instead we had to call Lilliput and all Lilliputians 'the enemy'.

But Zaya and me, we never gave up, no matter how cold and hungry we were. In the middle of the night we burrowed a hole under the wall, stole a boat and rowed across to Lilliput, where we found a warm welcome, where Gran Baruta and Tapit took us in, looked after us, and the whole island adopted us, as they adopt all of us who have managed to escape from Blufescu. To everyone on Lilliput, a stranger is a friend.

But our escape had not gone unnoticed on Blufescu. The hole in the wall was discovered. A boat had been stolen. The emperor Bronar spread it about all over Blufescu that two children had been kidnapped by the Lilliputians, that the Lilliputians were child-snatchers, and a threat to every child on Blufescu. He told the people that soon his mighty warships would sail over to Lilliput, and rescue the two kidnapped children of Blufescu, that right was on their side, that Lilliput must be conquered, that the enemy over there open their eggs round end first, which meant they were wicked and uncivilised, and anyway they had no right to be there, that many years before they had stolen Lilliput from Blufescu, whose people were superior in every way because they ate their eggs from the sharp end first.

Bronar had more than a hundred ships in the

harbour, all the guns and sailors he needed. He knew that we had no warships, only a small fishing fleet, and that no one on Lilliput ever carried weapons – Gulliver's Law, we call it. Gran Baruta and Tapit and the council went across the channel to talk to him, to try to reason with him. But he would not listen. He told them that he was emperor of both islands, and he could come across the sea, with a fleet of warships, and occupy Lilliput whenever he pleased.

And then he came, Son of Gulliver, Owzat, our Mountain Man. He was why Bronar's ships stayed in the harbour, why the invasion did not come. That was why he was needed. His coming was like a miracle for us.

CHAPTER TWENTY-ONE

Come What May

J.J. was brushing the tears from her cheeks. Zaya and Natoban were looking to me now to take up the story again.

So I did.

I made up my mind what to do then and there, after Natoban told me everything about Blufescu, about the emperor Bronar. I was not brave. I was angry, angry that my Lilliputian friends, the kindest, most fair-minded and most generous people I had ever met, might soon be enslaved by this tyrant across the water. Something had to be done. And wasn't I called Son of Gulliver?

I would do as he had done all those years before, as
he would do if he were here now.

I remember looking out to sea towards Blufescu that
same evening. The water in the channel seemed dark
and deep, the waves rolling in towards me. I could not
swim. But I knew Gulliver had swum across before me.
Son of Gulliver would go where he had gone. Come
what may, I would do what my father had done.

I said nothing of what I had in mind to Zaya and
Natoban. I said nothing to Baruta or Tapit, nothing to
anyone except Mother. I lay awake for a long time that
night, telling her what I was going to try to do the next
day. I was more worried about crossing the sea than
anything else, I told her. I knew it was too deep out in
the middle for me to be able to wade all the way across.
After all, even Gulliver, a full-grown man, had found
himself out of his depth, and been forced to swim. And
I could not swim. I had an idea that might work, I told
her, but I knew I could be in trouble if it didn't, because I
had seen how rough it could be out there in the channel
between the islands. I was far less worried by anything

the emperor Bronar, and his Blufescuan army, could do
to me when I got there – however many there were of
them. They'd be the same size as the Lilliputians, so no
threat to me at all.

I set off very early the next morning before anyone
on Lilliput was stirring – it was in the half-dark – and
found just what I was looking for, tied up to the quayside
in the harbour: two of the biggest fishing boats I could
have hoped for. I untied the ropes and waded out of
the harbour, towards the open sea, hauling the fishing
boats behind me. By this time some of the islanders

had woken up and spotted what I was doing. They came hurrying out of their houses and running down to the harbour, shouting at me to come back. I lifted a hand, waved to them cheerily and waded on.

The sea was soon up over my knees, up to my waist, then over my chest, and still I was only halfway across. I would need my fishing boats. When I found my feet were hardly touching the bottom and I could no longer walk, I put my plan into action. Holding the fishing boats out in front of me, one in each hand, and grasping them firmly, I lay in the water and let the

boats float me across, kicking hard with my legs to help propel myself. Time and again, the waves washed over my head, into my mouth, but my fishing boats kept me afloat just long enough. I kept kicking and kicking, until at last I felt my toes were touching rocks and seaweed below me. I could walk again. Ahead I could see the harbour of Blufescu, and behind it the great high wall the emperor had built all around the island. Both the harbour and the wall, and all the warships, were lined with men. They had seen me coming. They were ready for me. As I came closer I could see they were certainly not there

to welcome me. They were all armed, with bows and arrows, with spears and swords, and muskets too.

There were hundreds of them, thousands maybe, and their war cries were shrill and angry, and deafening. Each of them may have been small, but in these numbers they were terrifying, even though I knew they could not harm me. I did not want to harm them either. That was not what I was there for. It was the fleet of warships in the harbour that I was after.

As I came wading waist-deep into the harbour I found myself in range of the showers of falling arrows

they were shooting at me. Each arrow was just a pinprick, but too many were finding their target, on my legs and arms, on my face and neck. It was like being stung by insects all over. I feared some of the arrows might hit me in the eyes, and held up my hand to protect them. With the other hand I reached down and grabbed handfuls of anchor chains from the decks of the warships, and began to haul as many of them as I could out of the harbour. Everywhere sailors were abandoning their warships, leaping overboard in their hundreds.

Once out in the open sea, I let the warships go, and left them to drift away. Then I waded back into the harbour on Blufescu to fetch some more of them. I made the journey several times in and out of the harbour, each time under a shower of arrows, and there were musket balls and cannon balls bouncing off me too. Some of those did hurt, but not enough to trouble me much. And all the time the Blufescuans were shaking their fists at me, yelling at me, cursing me.

Soon all the warships were clear of the harbour, and drifting away out to sea. I was herding them like a flock of sheep, jumping up and down, slapping the water and making great waves that were driving them on, some on to the rocks, some further out to sea.

All along the shores of Lilliput the people were cheering and waving. I could hear a distant chanting, echoing over the ocean: 'Owzat! Owzat! Owzat!'

But I had not yet finished with Emperor Bronar and his soldiers. This tyrant of an emperor had driven these dear friends of mine, Zaya and Natoban, from their home, made orphans of them, and enslaved all the people of Blufescu. I determined I would set them free.

I waded back into the harbour and came up on to the shore. I saw the soldiers throwing down their weapons and scattering. I picked up all the bows and swords and muskets I could and hurled them into the water. I roared and raged and stamped, as only angry giants can – it was all I had to do – until most of the soldiers ran away. Those that were left were on their knees holding their hands up in surrender. I told them I would not hurt them, that they had nothing to fear from me. I was roaring no more by now. There was no need.

CHAPTER TWENTY-TWO

No More Tyrants!

The people of Blufescu were all watching me now, fearful of what I might do next.

They were at my mercy, and they knew it. As I strode through the streets of the town I found I could see well enough over the great wall. One look was enough. Everything Zaya and Natoban had told me had been true. I could see for myself now what this tyrant had done to his people. The countryside behind the wall was a scene of devastation. Nothing was left but ruins and dereliction. The people there were hiding where they could, looking up at me terrified. All of them were thin, and pale and dirty, their clothes in tatters. And there in the middle of the island surrounded by a great moat was the emperor's palace. I knew what to do with that.

I set about pulling that palace down, wall by wall, room by room, and then I trampled on it. This took me a while, and as I was finishing I heard behind me a giant cheer. I saw the enslaved people of Blufescu charging towards the great stone wall that surrounded the island. They had ladders, they had hammers, and they were angry. Soon they were knocking it down with anything they could find. Some were sitting up there astride the wall and pulling away the stones with their bare hands. I went to help them. Between us we flattened that great wall to the ground in a few hours, leaving in its place nothing but scattered stones, strewn everywhere. Nothing was left standing.

Afterwards, we all stood there breathless and exhausted, but all of us laughing, exultant with joy, the joy of freedom. No one ever discovered where the emperor Bronar and his cronies went. And no one cared. He was gone – that was all that mattered. When I left the island of Blufescu that evening, I left it as their friend. No one feared me. No one feared anyone. I told them all that their brothers and sisters across the water in Lilliput were longing to be friends with them again, and they told me they felt the same.

I walked and swam back to Lilliput with the help of my two fishing boats, and arrived back to a hero's welcome. Gran Baruta was there on the quayside to greet me, but I could see she was not at all happy.

'It was a very foolish thing you did,' she told me. 'You could have drowned out there in the channel. You may have saved us, but it was still very foolish. I was very worried, we all were. We never want any harm to come to you.' She was smiling up at me now. 'You know what you have done today, Son of Gulliver? You have conquered fear, driven it away, and brought us our peace again. It's a wonderful thing you have given us.'

Back in my house, lying on my bed that evening, Zaya and Natoban stayed with me, didn't you? You pulled all the arrows out of me – and there were hundreds of them – and then rubbed me all over with marigold ointment, which stung me at first but then soothed me. When they left that night I was ready for sleep. I had a lot I wanted to tell Mother, mostly about my plans for all those scattered stones on Blufescu, but I was so tired that I fell asleep almost at once.

CHAPTER TWENTY-THREE

Be There, Please, Mother

'Our turn,' Zaya said, tweaking my earlobe again, quite insistently. 'We know the rest as well as you do, Owzat.'

'We were there, remember? At the great gathering,' Natoban went on, tweaking my other earlobe. 'So we can tell it now.'

And between them, they did. Zaya first.

It was the best idea Owzat ever had, the best thing he ever did. The very next day everyone on Lilliput got in fishing boats and sailed over to Blufescu – Owzat wading across ahead of us. The people on Blufescu greeted us like long-lost friends. And then we did it, did it together. All of us Lilliputians and Blufescuans, we began to build Owzat's bridge – all his idea. We used the scattered stones from the palace and built a causeway from Blufescu over the sea to Lilliput. Even with Owzat's help, it took weeks and months, but we did it.

So now the two islands were joined, and everyone could come and go as they pleased.

It was Natoban's turn.

Not long afterwards, the people of both islands held a great gathering on the Cricket Field – as we all called it. Everyone was there. It began with a scrambled-egg feast. Gran Baruta stood up and told everyone: 'Never again, not for eggs or for anything else, will we ever break the peace between Lilliput and Blufescu. We shall fish together, trade with one another, be friends again as we always were for hundreds of years. We shall come and go from island to island freely, and tell our children our story of the coming of Gulliver, and now the story of the Son of Gulliver. There will be no more walls, no more tyrants. Never again will we be strangers to one another.'

Great cheers went up from all around. Gran Baruta held up her hand. 'Three hundred years ago, Gulliver brought us peace. And now this Son of Gulliver, this Owzat as some of you love to call him, has done the same. They both came to us with a warning of what tyranny and greed and war can do, how strangers can so easily become enemies – they have seen it in their own world, with their own eyes. Their world will be the world of our future, if we do not listen to them. We have seen how it can happen. This Son of Gulliver has reminded us of everything Gulliver told us, that we should always live for one another, that when we abandon kindness and understanding, cruelty and fear will take their place.'

Zaya took up the story.

The whole island seemed to have fallen quite silent as Gran Baruta was speaking. There was no sound of wind or waves, no birdsong even. It was as if the land itself and every creature that lived there were listening.

But this was when Gran Baruta told us something that saddened everyone on Lilliput, and Natoban and me more than anyone else. 'You all know from the story of Gulliver,' Gran Baruta said, 'that I tell on Gulliver's Day, under the blossoming apple tree, how he spent only a few years with us, and then left us because he missed his wife and his family and wanted to return to his own country. You all know how we built him a boat big enough so that he could sail safely home.

'Well – and I am so sad to have to tell you this – I have discovered that Owzat, our dear Son of Gulliver, has a great longing inside him to go to find his long-lost mother again. As you know, Zaya and Natoban have been guardians, good companions and best of friends to our Son of Gulliver ever since he came to Lilliput. Often, at night-times, they have heard him talking aloud to his mother, who is waiting for him far away across the seas in England. They have heard him telling her how much he loves living here on Lilliput with us all, how much he loves us, but also how he longs to go home and see her again. He told her often, they told me, how he could not leave the people of Lilliput and Blufescu until he was quite sure that this was a lasting peace between them. And they also heard him telling her that anyway he did not know how he could ever find a boat big enough to carry him across the sea to England.

'It was Zaya and Natoban who suggested to me that we should do what our ancestors did before us for Gulliver, and together build a great boat for our Son of Gulliver. We do not want him to go, of course – Zaya and Natoban least of all. But he has a mother he longs to be with again. We all know he has been a dear friend, the best of friends, to all of us here, on both our islands. He gave us back our peace. So I think we should help him find his mother, don't you?'

Everyone stood up then and clapped and cheered, all of us happy we had our peace again, but sad at heart because we knew you would be leaving us.

That night lying on your bed – and both of us were there to hear it – you told your mother in England that a boat was going to be built by the people of Lilliput and Blufescu, and that you would be coming home, that you would see her soon in England, in Fore Street, Mevagissey.

We heard you, Owzat, calling to her and calling – so loud she could have heard it far, far away: 'I am coming home to you across the sea,

Mother. I am coming home to England, to Fore Street, Mevagissey. Fore Street. Mevagissey. Be there, please, Mother. Be there.'

CHAPTER TWENTY-FOUR

I Am Coming, Mother

As Zaya finished, Natoban was turning my face towards his, his eyes looking deep into mine. 'Your mother will be there, Owzat; she will be there. You have to believe she will be there, waiting for you.'

'I believed it,' I told him, 'and I believe it still.'

Zaya tapped my arm. I could tell she was passing the story back to me, and I could tell too that J.J. was longing to hear it, to hear how our story joined her story, how our boat had met hers out there on the wide ocean.

'My time on Lilliput was coming to an end . . .' I began.

It was a strange time. I wanted to leave and yet I

didn't want to leave. I seemed to have spent my last few months on the island, as the boat was being built for me, learning and teaching, learning more English, and teaching cricket. Gran Baruta decided that even after all this time with them my English was not good enough, that by the time I reached England I should be able to speak the language as well as she could, as well as everyone could on Lilliput. So every day now she, and Tapit too, gave me lessons.

I loved my lessons with them because, as it turned out, these became two-way classes. They were anxious whilst I was with them to learn as much of my language as they could – so that in the end we could have a conversation in which I spoke English and they spoke Pashto.

We wrote nothing down. They did not seem at all interested in the written word. There were, as I had discovered, no books on Lilliput. 'We do not need them,' Gran Baruta once told me. 'Gulliver told us all about books, but we told him that on Lilliput we believe words are for speaking as air is for breathing. Air gives us only life, the spoken word gives us stories and life.'

But if I'm honest, teaching cricket to the children of Lilliput and Blufescu was my chief joy. We had cleared a field now on Blufescu and made a pitch over there too – which quickly became known as Owzat's Cricket Field. So now we could play on Lilliput and on Blufescu, home games and away games. Every game we played drew huge crowds.

The wicket was more bumpy on Blufescu than on Lilliput, so the Lilliputian children did not like it much over there because the ball bounced awkwardly. But crossing the stone causeway across the sea was always an adventure, for all the children on both islands. They loved 'walking on the sea' as they called it.

The Blufescuan children took to the game quickly and were soon playing just as well as the Lilliputians. In these early games, I always mixed the children up

so there was not too much island rivalry between them. I could nip arguments in the bud. None of them argued with the umpire, with me – I was too big. And these two always came with me, didn't you? Natoban helped me coach the children – he bowled as fast as

anyone, but not always accurately. And Zaya, although she did not like cricket at all, was there alongside me, was always with me too, helping to explain the rules to the little ones, and calming things down quickly before any quarrels could bubble up.

I think it was these cricket games between the

children, as much as anything, as much as the new causeway itself, that brought the two islands so quickly together again after the bad times, after living so long apart. Parents and grandparents, aunts and uncles, came across the channel to watch, got talking together, laughing together. Old hurts were forgotten or forgiven. New friends were made. Old friends discovered one another again.

And the boatbuilding helped too. The sailmakers from both islands came together on Blufescu, to work on the sails for my boat. They had not made sails this huge before – they had to build special sail lofts on Blufescu to accommodate them. It all took many skilled hands and a very long time. But Lilliputians and Blufescuans worked in the sail lofts on Blufescu together, side by side, to get them ready.

Meanwhile on Lilliput – where there were many more fully grown trees than on Blufescu ready to be felled – the boatbuilders from both islands gathered in the harbour every day to make a boat. The biggest boat that had been made on the islands, Gran Baruta told us, since the one that had been built all those years before for Gulliver. Her grandfather himself, she told me proudly, had helped to build that one. He had once walked the whole length of her. That boat measured over four hundred of his steps.

I could help to carry some of the timber from the forest to the harbour, but that was all I could do. I was no boatbuilder. Every day I would watch my boat taking shape above the slipway in the harbour on Lilliput. Impressed as I was with all the skill and hard work I was witnessing, how the people from both islands were cooperating so well in the building of it, I was worried. Half the forest on the island had already been cut down to build the boat, and yet I could already see that when it was finished it would be no more than a large rowing boat, less than half the length of the rubber dinghy that had only just held together long enough to bring me to Lilliput four years before. I could not tell them, after all their hard work, that to go to sea in such a small

boat, however well built, to face the towering waves of the open ocean was not likely to end well.

Neither could I tell Mother at night-times of my anxieties, just in case these two, Zaya and Natoban, my two eavesdropping friends here, were listening outside again – and anyway I did not want to worry her. This may sound silly, I know. But during my years on Lilliput, hope had turned to belief. Even though she had never once replied to me, there were times when I had truly come to believe that Mother really was hearing every word I spoke to her. She may have been hundreds of miles away, but I was sure she was listening to me. So I kept my worst fears to myself. I told no one.

But Zaya and Natoban, these two dear friends on my shoulders, these two knew me too well by now for me to be able to pretend. They knew my fears. They kept reassuring me that my boat was going to be so well made, so big, that no wave could overturn her, that she would be unsinkable. They were with me that great day, as I stood watching the boat being launched, as she slid down the slipway into the water, as the rudder was installed in its place, the mast raised and the sails brought out and set for the first time. She was strong and sturdy, and she was made with love and care. She would not sink, I told myself, she could not, she must not.

Everyone was there to witness the launch that day. Gran Baruta named the boat *Gulliver*, to thunderous cheers from all around the harbour. And Zaya said to me, I remember, from exactly where she is now, sitting up on my left shoulder: 'Don't worry, Owzat, she may be small but she will float. She will dance over the waves. Do not worry. She will carry you wherever you want to go.'

Thousands of voices were cheering that day, chanting my name, 'Owzat! Son of Gulliver! Owzat!'

I looked down at the brave little boat with her wonderfully carved prow, her oars waiting for me, and her white sail set high and whipping and clapping in the wind. She was ready to go, but the truth was that *I* was far from ready to go.

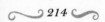

Day after day Zaya and Natoban took me out in the boat, and showed me how to row, how to hoist the sail, how to tack with the wind, to use the rudder.

They showed me how to steer into the waves, warned me never to be caught sideways by a big one. They taught me not to be afraid of the sea, but to know her and respect her and understand her.

What a gift the islanders had made me. What work they had put into it. But I had known all along of course that this was a parting gift, and that was troubling me more and more. My longing to leave was growing daily, as was my reluctance to go. I kept telling myself, and Zaya and Natoban, that I was only waiting for a fair wind and for the seas to calm. But I think they knew how much I was dreading leaving them, and leaving Lilliput, where I had been so loved, where I had grown up and become tall, where there were no strangers, where the people lived for one another, and for peace – and where they loved cricket too. It was a world I loved.

There were still days when I made up my mind to stay, that this was the place for me forever, that these were the people I would live amongst all my life. I knew I would be returning to a very different kind of world altogether. In the end, it was only Mother who made me decide to go. One night as I lay in my bed, thinking of her, of Father, of Hanan, I was sure I could hear her voice in my head. I was trying to explain to her how difficult I was finding it to bring myself to leave. And then she spoke to me. She was telling me she had been waiting every day for me to come, longing to see me again, to hear my voice.

'I'm coming, Mother,' I called to her, called out loud. 'I am coming! I promise. I will leave tomorrow!' I just hoped Zaya and Natoban were not listening outside.

I wanted no one to know, especially these two, because I could not face saying my goodbyes. I would creep out at dawn, go down to the boat and sail away. It would be better that way. But when I stepped outside my house the next morning, Zaya and Natoban were there waiting for me.

CHAPTER TWENTY-FIVE

Homeward Bound

'We overheard him,' Zaya told J.J. 'We were there the evening before listening outside the window. We heard every word.'

'And we told everyone,' Natoban added.

'Which was why they were all waiting for us down at the harbour,' I went on . . .

. . . All the fishing boats from Blufescu and Lilliput were there, filling the harbour, all of them crammed with little people, all of them silent. Gran Baruta was there on the harbourside, Tapit at her side.

'Listen all around you,' she said. 'It is the sound of our silence, and our silence speaks a thousand words, words of love, and thanks. Go, Son of Gulliver, go safe. Go east always, towards the rising sun, as Gulliver did. He was not just a good man, but a fine navigator too. He had sailed the world. He knew these things. Go east, dear Son of Gulliver. And come back whenever you want to. You will always have a home here. We will tell your story to our children and they will tell it to their children. You will never be forgotten.'

For a while, I had no voice to reply.

Then, all I could think to say was: 'And one day I will tell your story too.'

I looked around for Zaya and Natoban – to say goodbye to them – but they were nowhere to be seen. In a way I was glad of it. These two good companions, who had hardly left my side all these years, had not been just guardians, but my family. I had a brother now, and another sister. Just to see them at that moment might have been enough to change my mind.

Maybe they knew that.

*

'We did, big brother,' said Zaya.

'Yes. We did,' agreed Natoban. 'We knew.'

As I stepped into the boat I saw that she was piled at one end, under the shelter, with provisions of all kinds, and at the other end she was stacked with barrels of water. There was barely room in the middle of the boat for me to sit down and row. I looked up at the crowd that lined the harbour, the children, my cricketing children, sitting on the walls, their faces filled with sadness. I had to say something else to them, and I could think of only one word to say. I lifted my hat, then with a great shout of 'Owzat!' I threw it high in the air.

The sadness all around me turned at once to laughter. The silence broke into echoing cheers of 'Owzat! Owzat!'

I took to my oars and rowed my way through all the boats that had crowded into the harbour. I went carefully, for one knock from my sturdy rowing boat

would have sunk any one of them. In front of me, all around me, the little people were scattering petals and flowers on the water. I rowed out of the harbour through a sea of colour of orange and magenta; and then, once clear of the little boats, I began to pull hard for the open ocean.

The last I heard of the little people of Lilliput and Blufescu, they were singing, and faint though it was, I could just make out Mother's lullaby song, my song, their song now. But in no time at all I could hear them no longer, nor see them. They were gone. Soon enough the two islands were no more than two distant shadows on the horizon, then one shadow. Then nothing. I was out on the open sea, alone.

CHAPTER TWENTY-SIX

So Here We Are

There was a good breeze. So I decided to ship my oars and sail by the wind. I wasn't having to try to remember everything Zaya and Natoban had taught me in my sailing lessons. I was doing everything instinctively – you were good teachers, you two. This vast empty sea, which had once held such terrors for me on my last voyage, was no longer my enemy. She was giving me her wind, and her waves and her tide. She was helping me home.

But I was already regretting that I had not given myself the chance to say a proper goodbye to my two best friends, when I thought I heard the voice of Zaya calling me. Then I was hearing two voices. They were calling me together. I was quite sure at first I was imagining their voices, that it must be the wind in the sails, or some seabird, or that my ears were playing tricks on me. But wind, I thought, doesn't whistle in words. And birds don't speak in words. I was hearing words, real words!

I was hearing, 'Owzat! Owzat! Son of Gulliver!' And: 'Fore Street, Mevagissey, Fore Street, Mevagissey.'

Then I saw them both climbing up my legs, out from amongst the water barrels and on to my knees. There they were, standing there, laughing, and then I was laughing with them. It was such a reunion. I was full of questions and they were full of answers.

'Our turn, our turn!' Natoban cried, shushing me. 'We asked Gran Baruta,' he explained to J.J. 'It was Zaya's idea. She said you weren't a good enough sailor to go out on your own. And I agreed. So did Gran Baruta. "Go and look after him," she told us, "as he has looked after us."'

'So here we are,' Zaya said, joining in. 'And the three of us sailed away, always towards the east, just as

Gulliver had done before, waking every morning to look for land on the horizon, land that we hoped would soon be England. We had days of perfect weather, stiff breezes and no storms. We sped along under a full sail, hearts full of hope, happy to be together. We saw dolphins, we saw flying fish, we saw gannets. All was going so well.'

Natoban, I could see, was aching to take over the story again. They talked over each other for a while, but Zaya was not giving way to him. 'But then one afternoon,' she said, 'the waves began to heave, and the wind got up, and the clouds were gathering, and the thunder was roaring. The world darkened around us, and lightning lit up the night sky. Our little boat rode the waves well, but the sea was coming in over the side more and more all the time. All night Owzat clung to the rudder, doing all he could to keep the bow into the towering waves, climbing up so steeply sometimes that we thought we must overturn. We were hanging on for dear life. All the time the boat was filling, and was lower and lower in the water. Natoban and I, we stayed deep inside the pocket of your coat. We wanted to get out, to help, but you said

it was too dangerous and we had to stay where we were. And it was true of course, the smallest wave could have swept us overboard.'

We told the last of our story together – the three of us in turn.

'And it was just as well,' I said, 'that you were deep down in my pocket, because when at last it did happen, and the boat was knocked over, at least we were together. I managed to cling on to the side of the boat and somehow found the strength to right it. I hauled myself up. I thought I'd lost you both, till you crawled laughing and spluttering out of my pocket. We just lay there in the bottom of the boat, exhausted, and holding on to one another, frightened to let go.'

'We were alive, but only just,' Natoban went on. 'All our food and water were gone. The mast and the sail were gone. We'd lost our oars. We were lying there waiting for the next big wave that would finish us, waiting for the end.'

'We held you close,' said Zaya, 'And you held us close.'

'These two were both drifting in and out of sleep,' I

told J.J. 'I remember thinking we would all of us drown in our sleep, and never wake again. I would not see Mother, so she would never know how hard we had tried to get to England to Fore Street, Mevagissey, to find her. I was filled with sorrow at the thought of Mother and Uncle Said, and how they would be waiting for me all their lives and how I would never come. But at least, I thought, we three friends were doing this together. We would die together, and there was comfort in that, great comfort.'

CHAPTER TWENTY-SEVEN

Yellow as the Sun

The next thing I knew, Zaya and Natoban were yelling at me, pinching my earlobes, trying to shake me awake. There was sun on my face, warming wonderful sun. I sat up. The sea was like glass all around. Not a breath of wind. Our boat lay quite still in the water. And Zaya and Natoban were shouting at me to get up, to turn around, to look.

'Over there!' they were shouting. 'A boat, a boat! Look! Look!'

And there it was, a boat, no more than a stone's throw away across the water. There was music playing. She was a rowing boat, but bigger, much bigger than

ours, and there was a covered shelter at one end, like an open cabin. And she was yellow, bright yellow like the sun. And there was someone in the boat, someone in a bright yellow cagoule, as yellow as the boat.

And that was you, J.J. You were rowing across towards us. But you know that, don't you? So here we are, and that's our story.

FIFTH
Part

CHAPTER TWENTY-EIGHT

Anything But Ordinary

All the way through our story, J.J. had scarcely taken her eyes off us. She sat there, sometimes nursing her bandaged wrist, listening in amazement and wonder at everything we were telling her. She told me later that if Zaya and Natoban had not been there with me, she would not have believed a word of it. And they both told me later how, looking at J.J. during the story, they could never have ever imagined there could be another giant anywhere in the world as big as I was – and she was bigger. I had already warned them, on our voyage across the sea, that when we reached England they would find themselves in a land of giants, most of them far bigger than me. But J.J. was the first one of these giants they had met and they were in awe of her, as I was, especially when she told us how and why she happened to be there all alone out on the ocean.

She certainly had a very different way from me of telling a story. We had lived ours as we told it to her. I think all three of us were seeing it again in our minds. We weren't telling it in any way to make it more exciting. I knew I told it as I did because I wanted to remember it, remember everything and everyone. But she told hers in a very matter-of-fact way, as if what she was doing, all she had done, was the most normal thing in the world.

I think J.J. felt she had to tell her story, because we had told her ours. But she also explained that because we were all going to be on a small boat together for some while, we really ought to get to know something about her, about who she was and why she was there. Compared to our story, hers was quite ordinary, she said.

It was anything but ordinary. She began with her full name.

'My name is Jillian Forsyth Wood. A mouthful, isn't it? My dad always called me J.J., and I loved that. So I made everyone call me J.J. You see? Ordinary. You are Owzat, Son of Gulliver, or Mountain Man. You are Zaya and Natoban, and I am just plain J.J. I am nearly twenty-three years old – twenty-one when I left home. And I am here because of my dad. That sounds silly, doesn't it? We are all here because of our fathers and mothers. You, Omar, Owzat, Son of Gulliver, you are certainly out here in the ocean because of your mother. I am out here on this boat because of my father.

'I was at university when he became ill. Dad was the reason I always loved boats and rowing. When I was very little, he used to take me out on the river in a rowing boat – it was on the River Avon in Stratford, where we lived then. I loved rowing at once, took to it, he often said, like a duck to water. Then, a year or two later, when we went to live by the sea in Salcombe – that's in Devon – he'd take me out sailing. I was still quite young. He always said I could sail a boat before I could walk. Almost true but not quite.

Anyway, after that I discovered I was only truly happy when I was out on the water, messing about in boats, any boats, sailing, rowing, didn't matter.

'At university I was supposed to be studying law, but I preferred to be out there rowing with my friends on the river. I loved racing against other crews, eight of us pulling together, powering through the water. And it turned out I was becoming quite good at it, good enough to win races, good enough in the end to row in my university crew. I was so happy, on cloud nine.

'Then Dad got ill. The doctors told us that he would not live for long. And they were right. Dad died the day before my big race, on the Thames in London it was. I rowed my heart out for him and we won. But I discovered that day that winning isn't enough, that other things are more important. I made up my mind what I had to do and promised myself that I would do it.

'One of Dad's doctors told me that if they were ever going to find a cure for Dad's illness they needed all the money they could get, for research. So I decided I would raise thousands of pounds. I would do it for Dad. I only knew one way I could do it. I would row. I would find people and businesses to sponsor me, to help me, so I could provide the money we needed for the research. I decided I would be the first woman to row single-handed around the world. So that's what I've been doing now for over two years.

'I left England two years, seven months and two days ago. I know that because I've got this little book – a logbook we call it – and I write down in it every day where I am, how far I've gone, where I see land, what the weather is like, what weather is coming, which port in which country was my last stop, and which will be the next stop, how much water and food I have left, the birds I spot, the whales and dolphins I see, the wind direction and strength, the height of the waves, the current, everything that has broken on the boat and needs mending, the up days, the down days. It's all there in *Sunshine's* logbook.

'I call my boat *Sunshine*, after Dad's favourite

song, "Here Comes the Sun". He loved that song. And sometimes he would call me that too. I was J.J., I was Sunshine, and I was Jillian when he was cross with me. Which was hardly ever.

'I was counting the other day, as I was reading through my logbook. I've visited thirty-five countries,

been knocked over three times – turned upside down, and rolled back up again – been swept overboard five times, my lifeline on, luckily, so each time I could manage to climb back in again. I've bumped into rocks, into icebergs, a container, and once into a floating bed, and once into a whale. Well, I still think she bumped

into me. Her fault! And whilst I've never been badly hurt, I've got bumps and bruises all over me, strained this muscle, pulled that muscle, broken a finger and a toe, the same stupid toe three times.' She wiggled her toes. 'It's the one I can't wiggle. And now this.' She held up her bandaged wrist. I could see her fingers were swollen. 'I don't think I have properly broken it. But it's not good. It happened in the storm. I can move my fingers, look. Maybe it's a tendon that's torn . . . don't know. It doesn't hurt too much unless I'm using it. The trouble is, of course, that I have to use it a lot when I row. So I can't row, not far anyway. I could just about manage to row myself across to you when I woke up and saw your boat. But you weren't that far away. I can cook and wash myself, do most of what I need to do one-handed. But I can't row one-handed, because I've got two oars. And that's a pity, and that's a problem.

'The big problem is that we are still about fifty nautical miles away from the south coast of

England, and I know I can't row there. Dad always said I had to look on the bright side of life. When I was little and I was feeling down, he'd often sing me that song if I was feeling a bit miserable about something: "Always Look on the Bright Side of Life". Another of his favourite songs – Dad loved to sing. I think I must have sung that song hundreds of times in the last couple of years, whenever things looked bad, when a storm hit. And then, when it was over, and the world brightened and the sun came out, I'd be singing "Here Comes the Sun". One way or another my dad and his songs have been with me all round the world.

'Of course the bright side of hurting my wrist is that, if I hadn't done it, I would have been miles away by now, miles nearer to the coast of England, and then I wouldn't have been here when you came by, so I wouldn't have met you and you wouldn't have met me, and we wouldn't be sitting here in the middle of the ocean together telling each other our stories. So there you are, that's my story. Like I said, ordinary compared to yours, and shorter too!'

CHAPTER TWENTY-NINE

Your Home Too

As J.J. finished, I was thinking: how strange and wonderful it was that two such stories, hers and mine, should meet like this, by chance, and in the middle of thousands of miles of ocean, and that in a strange way our separate stories were now becoming one story, our story, and that none of us on that boat knew how this story would end. But I did know how I hoped it would end: in a café in Fore Street, Mevagissey, with Mother and Uncle Said there, waiting for me.

'Fore Street, Mevagissey,' I said to her. 'It's in England. Do you know it?'

'Well, I know Mevagissey,' she replied. 'I know Mevagissey quite well. I've sailed in there sometimes with Dad, from Salcombe – that's where we live, where I set out from when I began all this. It's just up the coast in Devon from Mevagissey. That's where I was heading for, Salcombe. In fact, when I think about it now, I reckon we're even closer where we are now to Mevagissey, than we are to Salcombe. But with my wrist as useless as it is, nowhere is close.

'Just before I found you, I was about to radio for help, but the last thing I want is for Sunshine to have to be towed into port on the end of a rope by a lifeboat. After all she's been through, Sunshine deserves to be rowed in, not towed in. It wouldn't be right; she wouldn't like it and I wouldn't like it. Not a good way to end my single-handed voyage round the world.' She laughed then, and went on. 'Funny that. I'm supposed to be rowing single-handed around the world – that's what they call it, single-handed – but I've discovered you really can't row single-handed at all, not far anyway. It's impossible. You just go round in circles if you try. And I've tried! One hand, one wrist, is not enough. So near, so far.'

I really hadn't thought of it, but Zaya had. They had both been sitting on my shoulders all through J.J.'s story, as intent on it as I had been. Zaya was whispering in my ear. 'You can row, Owzat,' she said. 'Tell her you can row.'

Natoban spoke for me. 'Owzat can row,' he said. 'He's quite good. And we can help.'

J.J. was looking at me.

'Well, I could try,' I told her. 'But I'm not that good at it, and this boat is big, much bigger than ours, and the oars are huge. I don't think I could manage both these oars.'

J.J. was smiling broadly. 'We could manage together maybe,' she said. 'And then we could row into Mevagissey. You wouldn't have to do it alone. You could take one oar and row two-handed, and I could row single-handed – if you see what I'm saying – on the other oar. But you'll have to pull hard, with all your strength, Owzat, otherwise we'll just go round in circles. That would be wonderful. And Zaya and Natoban, we'll need you too on lookout – for other boats, for land. That way I won't need to radio in for help, and that way my lovely boat, my *Sunshine*, won't have to be towed in by a lifeboat with everyone watching.

'And that's another problem. If they know I'm coming there'll be a lot of people waiting, a lot of fuss. But they'll be expecting me to come into Salcombe, not Mevagissey. That's what I'll tell them on the radio. We'll need to creep in quietly, under cover of dark, if we can. Best not be seen at all. Early morning is good, if wind and tide will let us do it.'

It was sad for us to have to abandon our brave little boat mid-ocean, and leave her all alone as we rowed away. Natoban and Zaya were especially upset. It was their last link to Lilliput. But it was the only thing we could do. She had been battered by the storm and was low in the water. She was only just afloat anyway. None of us wanted to stay to watch her sink, so we just rowed away from her and tried not to look back. But Natoban and Zaya could not resist several last looks behind them until the little boat disappeared from view. They were quiet after that for

a long while, and as sad as I'd ever seen them.

One-handed, single-handed she might have been, but J.J. rowed more strongly than I ever could two-handed. Every one of her strokes was long and powerful through the water. She would lean right forward, and then pull, digging just deep enough with her oar, judging each wave perfectly, so that her oar never skimmed or dug too deep as mine often did. It was hard to keep up with her, but I did my best.

It took six days of hard rowing into the wind and waves. Then one evening, Natoban, who was kneeling precariously on the bow, at last saw land ahead. 'England!' he cried. He jumped down then, took Zaya by the hand and together they did a joyful little jig in the bottom of the boat.

'England,' J.J. said, 'and Mevagissey, if we're lucky and my sat nav is right.' She was resting on her oar, and gazing at the twinkle of lights in the distance, like stars. 'Home,' she said. 'My home, your home too.'

CHAPTER THIRTY

Not Like Lilliput

The lights on shore came ever closer, as we drifted in through the night. J.J. did not want to hurry. She timed our arrival perfectly. The little town and its harbour were quiet and still as we came in. No one seemed to be about. We rowed slowly, dipping our oars as silently as we could. We passed several fishing boats on their moorings, and came up gently on to the shingle on the beach. J.J. lowered the anchor over the side, and let it slip into the water. We did not splash as we got out; we did not talk.

We had done all our talking before we arrived. J.J. had planned exactly what to say, what to do, where to go. She had explained everything to me.

Provided Mother had reported to the police and claimed asylum, as she should have done as soon as she arrived in England. Find Mother and all would be well, she said – then there should be no problem about me staying.

But I had to claim asylum as quickly as possible, to report to the first police officer we saw, or walk into the first police station. The worst thing was to try to run away, to hide, and then get caught. I could be locked up, she told me, put in detention, in prison even, and then sent back to Afghanistan. We had to do it right, or it could all go very wrong. And even if Mother wasn't there, Uncle Said would be, and being my only living relative and having lived in England for years and years, all should be well and I should be allowed to stay. She was sure of it. I was glad she was, because I understood very little of what she'd been saying about reporting to the police and claiming asylum. But I understood her well enough when she talked about how I could be locked up if I tried to run away and was caught.

'I like England. I love it in many ways,' J.J. told me. 'But it is not like Lilliput, I'm ashamed to say. We do not always welcome strangers as we should. Whatever happens, stay close to me, and whatever you do, don't run off. Just follow me.'

J.J. had googled a map of Mevagissey. She had found Fore Street. We knew where it was and how to find it. But even so, arriving in a strange place in the half-dark, it was not at all easy for us to find our way.

It was a small town gathered round its harbour, a few

small shops and cafés, the houses low, the windows small. Zaya and Natoban were in my pocket, peering out, as we made our way across the muddy shore, and up the slipway on to the quayside. I was thinking it must have been as strange to them as it was to me. But then I thought again. It was, in fact, quite like the harbour in Lilliput – just bigger to them, so much bigger.

Walking around the harbour now, and down through the streets of the town, I was beginning to feel more and more anxious.

There was a rubber dinghy below us in the harbour, and I remembered then the boat I had nearly died in, that so many *had* died in. What if Mother had been in a boat like that, in storms like that? What if? What if? Please God. Please God.

'This must be Fore Street,' J.J. whispered. 'We're nearly there.'

The street was narrow and silent. It was so hard to take in. This was Fore Street, Mevagissey. This was Mother and Uncle Said's street. As we walked along I was looking all the while up at all the darkened windows, willing Mother to be lying asleep in one of those rooms.

'Be up there, Mother,' I said to myself. 'Please God be up there.'

I had lived for this moment, been longing for it all this time. J.J. had stopped in front of a doorway.

'This is it,' she whispered. 'It's the only café in the street. They must live above it.' She was leaning forward then, trying to read a notice on the door. 'It's closed,' she said. 'But there's something else. It says it's for sale.' She was peering in the window. 'And look, there are no tables in there, no chairs, nothing. No one's there. The place is empty.'

CHAPTER THIRTY-ONE

You're That Girl, Aren't You?

We sat there on the harbour wall watching the dawn come up. There was nothing to say. Zaya and Natoban were staying out of sight, just as J.J. had told them to. One glimpse of them, and there would be a lot of impossible explaining to do – we all knew that. I did feel them moving about in my pocket, and I knew they must be peeking out at this new world about them, at the giants who were beginning to open up their shops, at the giants who were readying their fishing boats in the harbour, at the first cars and bicycles and motorbikes they had ever seen. Whenever I felt them I would push them back down, and whisper to them to stay there.

They did, but only for a while.

The town was slowly waking up around us. I watched the people coming and going; I felt more a stranger here amongst my fellow giants than I had ever felt in Lilliput. Then we saw that some of them were beginning to notice Sunshine down on the muddy beach below the quayside. A small crowd was gathering, walking around it, peering into it.

'I think we'd better go,' said J.J., getting to her feet.

'Go where?' I asked her.

'I'll tell you on the way,' she said. 'Come on.'

Walking away through the streets, with more and more people now hurrying past us towards the harbour to join the growing crowd, J.J. was explaining everything. 'We have to find the police station, but I'm not sure if there is one in Mevagissey. We have to go and report to a policeman as soon as we can. You have to claim asylum properly, otherwise you will be illegal, an illegal immigrant – I told you, remember? We don't want you ending up in a detention centre or prison, or being sent back to Afghanistan, do we? I know you want to find your mother and Uncle Said, but that may not be easy now. So even before we do that, we must report to a police station to tell them you are here. Don't worry. I'll look after you. Stay close now.'

We turned into a dark alleyway, where there was no one about. Then J.J. was crouching down beside me to talk to Zaya and Natoban. 'And you two had better hide away in my pocket now. They'll search Omar, but they won't search me. I can explain all about him when we find a police station. But I can't explain away you two. Not in a million years!' She took one of them in each hand and slipped them into the pocket of her cagoule. 'And for goodness' sake, keep your heads down,' she told them. 'Keep quiet. Not a peek, not a squeak, you hear?'

We walked around for some time, before J.J. asked a lady who was opening up her café where the police station was in Mevagissey. I looked away because the woman kept staring at me, and it was not a welcoming stare.

'No police station here,' she told J.J. 'You'll have to go to St Austell. Miles away. Nice yellow sailing cagoule you've got. You've come in on a boat by the looks of you. Him too?' She was still staring at me when I looked up. But then I saw she had caught sight of something over my shoulder. 'Well I never, there's a stroke of luck: a police car.' She waved the police car down.

There were two police officers inside. She went over and was having a word with them, looking back at us from time to time. The car doors opened and the two police officers got out, putting on their caps. They were walking towards us. I felt like running, but J.J. had me by the arm, and was holding me tight. Then she was telling them who she was and who I was and how she had found me out on the open sea in a boat, all alone, and brought me here. Holding up her bandaged wrist, she was explaining how without my help she could never have gone on rowing and reached the coast.

The two police officers were both agog at her story. She went on, all about Uncle Said and my mother who should have been living in Fore Street, and how

they kept a café there. She told them how she had been
rowing single-handed around the world for over two
years, and that although she hadn't been able to finish
exactly how she wanted, nor in Salcombe as she intended,
how she was pleased to be home, and pleased to be in

Mevagissey. 'We are trying to find a police station,' she went on. 'My friend Omar needs to claim asylum.'

When she finished, one of the police officers said, 'I know you, don't I?'

And the other said, 'You're that J.J. or something or other. You're that girl, aren't you? You're that girl on the telly, in the papers. I've seen you. You've been rowing round the world for your dad, haven't you?'

'Yes, that's me,' J.J. told them. She changed the subject quickly. 'Now about my friend's mother and his Uncle Said – he's a British citizen, been living here for years – we couldn't find them in the café in Fore Street where they were supposed to be. We went there. It's empty. Up for sale.'

'That's right,' said the other police officer. 'I used to go in there. Nice place, nice people, good coffee, great sticky buns. They closed it.'

'They left,' the lady said, who still hadn't gone away. 'I know them. They haven't moved far. They've got that new fish and chip café down on the harbour. Owzat, they call it. Good name. Nice people. And it's a good chippy too. Old Said does all the frying and she looks after the customers. Best food in town I reckon. She's your mother then, dear?' she said, being a lot more kindly towards me now than before.

'First things first,' one of the police officers said. 'I'm afraid we'll have to keep the boy with us, take him back to the station. We have to inform the immigration people, take his details, and all that. You come with us, lad. We'll look after you.'

I was running before anyone could stop me, before I knew myself what I was going to do.

They shouted at me but I was gone. There was no way I was going with them. I knew J.J. had told me not to run. But I had to. I had to find Mother.

CHAPTER THIRTY-TWO

A Safe Place

Somehow I found my way back through the myriad little streets and down to the harbour. By now there were hundreds of people there, lining the harbour walls, and more crowds down on the beach, all clustering around *Sunshine*, walking round her and touching her, bending over, taking pictures and selfies.

Then I saw the name in big gold letters above the windows of a fish and chip café. 'Owzat'.

And there they were! Mother and Uncle Said were standing side by side in the crowd by the harbour wall outside the café. I stopped running. I needed time to think, to make up my mind what to say. They were looking down over the quayside at *Sunshine*, like everyone else. They still hadn't seen me.

They didn't notice me until I was right beside them, until I spoke.

I spoke to her first in Pashto, then in English. '*Mor*,' I said. 'Mother, I've been looking for you, and you haven't been easy to find.'

She was older, her hair whiter. I did not want to let her go. She kept holding my face in her hands and kissing me. She could not speak for crying, and neither could I.

Then she was pushing me away from her, taking me by the shoulders and turning me round. Standing in front of me was Hanan, still taller than me, Hanan, my beautiful sister – alive, alive!

We were still hugging some time later when the police officers arrived with J.J. I saw there was movement shifting inside her cagoule pocket. I was willing Zaya and Natoban to do as they had been told and keep their heads down. They kept their heads down too, whilst everyone in the crowd was beginning to realise who this young woman was in the yellow cagoule. The news was spreading fast around the harbour. People came running from all over. There was cheering and clapping, and soon the phones were out, and everyone wanted to take photos. Then she was being carried around the harbour on the shoulders of a couple of burly bearded fishermen.

We were in the fish and chip café, with Mother and Hanan and Uncle Said and one of the police officers, when J.J. came back a while later and found us. The other police officer was with her. She patted her pocket reassuringly and nodded at me. She told us that it had all been arranged with the police and the immigration people, that I could stay with Mother and Uncle Said whilst everything was sorted out and all the right paperwork was done. Then the TV and radio people arrived. There were cameras flashing and clicking, and endless interviews in the fish and chip café with J.J. and with me. She was the hero of the hour. She was the one who had rowed all around the world, the first woman ever to do it.

But all the time she made out to them that I was the hero, that without me she would never have got home. She told them all she had hurt her wrist and could not row, and how we had rowed the last fifty miles together, and how glad she was that I had found my family, and found a home with them here in Mevagissey, in a safe place where there was peace, where people were kind, and where she knew people were kind to strangers.

Then she said, and only four of us there know why she said it – Zaya, Natoban, J.J. and me – 'I think we all have to live for one another, don't you?'

CHAPTER THIRTY-THREE

A Proper Home

So that's how I come to be writing this now, many years later, sitting in my room above the fish-and-chip café, looking over the harbour in Mevagissey. I play cricket for the local team and can hit the ball harder, and bowl faster, than any of them. They call me Tiny – again! – but I don't mind. I long to tell them sometimes that I was once a giant in another place, a boy giant, but a giant in a different world. They'll know when the book comes out, if it ever comes out.

I spend my days out at sea with Hanan in Uncle Said's fishing boat. Mevagissey is our proper home. The café is a proper family business. Hanan and I fish the fish – crab, lobster, herring, mackerel, sole – but mostly cod and haddock because fish and chips is by far the most popular choice on our menu.

Uncle Said cooks behind the counter – he likes to sing as he cooks; he sings croakily as he sizzles!

And Mother and Hanan look after the customers in the café. Their English is terrible, Uncle Said's is better. But mine is perfect, though some people say I speak in rather a strange old-fashioned kind of way, as people might have spoken in England hundreds of years ago. Lilliputian English, old-fashioned? How dare they!

And as for Zaya and Natoban, still my two best friends in all the world, in both the worlds I have lived in, I still see them from time to time, but not at home, not in Mevagissey, not any more. And thereby hangs another story.

To begin with they tried to live with me up here in my room, where they were safe enough from the cats and dogs that wandered the streets outside, from the gulls that were quite capable of picking them up and carrying them off, from the cars in the streets. They were safe, too, from giants who strode with their great heavy feet through those streets. I knew all too soon, as they did, that long-term this could be no life for them, imprisoned as they were in my room with me. I worried about them if ever I had to go out. Natoban in particular was longing to go out with me. He would spend long hours sitting at the window, gazing out to sea. They could not stay with us, I knew that. They needed a proper home, and I knew it could not be with me and Mother and Hanan and Uncle Said. They loved having them in the house – once they had got over the surprise of meeting them, once they knew their story and mine. They were part of the family now, but we all knew it could not last.

The days they looked forward to most were Mondays when the café was closed, and we would all go out in Uncle Said's rickety old car that smells of fish. Our favourite trip was to Zennor, a little village not far away, where there was a high rocky moor, from where you could see the sea all around, a wild, windy empty place. We would often take a picnic up there. Zaya and Natoban and I could run off together, and we could all feel we were back on Lilliput again, and I could feel I was a giant again.

Then on one Monday evening, up on the moor above Zennor, Mother and Hanan and Uncle Said and I were packing up and getting ready go back home, when we realised the two little ones weren't with us. We called out for them, looked everywhere. I checked in the picnic basket they liked to ride in sometimes. But they were nowhere. We stayed until dark calling for them, and calling for them. Hanan and I were up on the moor all that night, searching for them, waiting for them, calling for them. Uncle Said drove back to Mevagissey and brought us back a tent and all we needed to sleep up there.

Night after night we were there. We were not going to leave without them. Hanan stayed with me most of the time, and Uncle Said and Mother would come out every morning when they could to look for them with us. We searched in amongst the rocks, along the banks of every stream, and climbed every hill on the moor again and again. My voice was hoarse with shouting, my eyes ached sometimes with crying. They were raw.

After two or three days I knew the worst must have happened. A fox had caught them, or a buzzard, or a stoat. Or they had strayed down on to the road and been run over, or maybe they had fallen into a pond, or perhaps they had got lost in a mist and wandered off the moor on to a farm, and a cat or a dog had taken them.

Day after day I came looking for them, week after week. J.J. would come over to help me whenever she could, from her home in Salcombe. Time and again she would come up to Zennor to help us look for them. I was giving up any hope of finding them, but J.J. never gave up on anything. She wasn't like that, and neither was Hanan. They would not let me give up and the search went on.

Both J.J. and Hanan were with me that morning. The three of us were lying awake in our tent. The wind was up. There was a strange sound outside. We thought at first it was the tent whipping and whining in the wind. We looked out. And there they were, Zaya and Natoban standing there, looking at us and smiling. They were not alone. Around them were gathered a dozen more little people, all of them staring at us. We stared back. 'Hello,' said Zaya. 'What are you doing up here?'

I was almost angry. 'Looking for you,' I told her.

'We're fine,' Natoban said. 'We've found some friends our own size. No cars up here, no dogs, no cats, and we can go where we want. We look after one another, just as we did on Lilliput.'

'Who are these people?' I asked him.

'They call themselves Spriggans,' Zaya told me. 'They've lived up here for thousands of years, long before giants like you came along. They know how to live amongst big people. They love stories like we do, and they've got lots of them to tell, and so have we. We're living up here with them now. Is that all right?'

I didn't know what to say for a while. 'Are you happy?' I asked them.

'Very,' said Zaya. 'They look after us very well. We look after each other. It's our home now. Don't worry about us. And you can come and see us any time you like.'

So that's what we did, what we still do. They found their world. I found mine. Different worlds they may seem to be, but they're not. We all live in the same world and I love it that way. I love the memories I have of Lilliput and Blufescu, I love the sea and the fishing, and all my family and friends in Mevagissey, and my dear Zaya and Natoban up on Zennor moor, and J.J.

One day, I want to row with her back to Lilliput to show her and Hanan the place where I lived, where I grew up. J.J. says she thinks she can work out where it is. She has a record of the longitude and latitude in her logbook, the exact spot in the ocean where we met by chance that day. She says all we would have to do is row due west from there, and sooner or later we would be bound to find Lilliput. It would be an adventure, she said, and she likes adventures. We'll take Zaya and Natoban with us, if they want to come. But that'll be another story, a whole other story, maybe for another book. It's got to happen first.

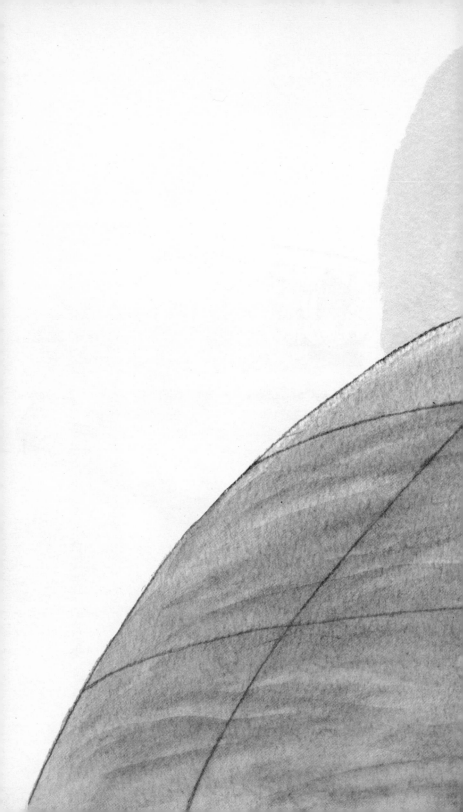